EMMANUEL CHABRIER

Emmanuel Chabrier

A l'ami Chabrier

FRANCIS POULENC

Emmanuel Chabrier

Translated by
CYNTHIA JOLLY

London
DENNIS DOBSON

Copyright 1961 by La Palatine, Geneva and Paris
English text copyright © 1981 by Dobson Books Ltd
Published in the original French under
this title by Editions La Palatine, Paris
All rights reserved

TO THE MEMORY OF
Ricardo Viñes and
Marcelle Meyer
unforgettable interpreters
of Chabrier

First published in Great Britain in 1981
by Dobson Books Ltd, 80 Kensington Church Street, London W8

Printed by Bristol Typesetting Co. Ltd,
Barton Manor, St. Philips, Bristol

ISBN 0 234 77252 2

Contents

Foreword	9
A Portrait of Chabrier	11
Life and Work	21
I. Childhood. Years of apprenticeship. L'Étoile – L'Education manquée	23
II. The Wagner Shock – Pièces pittoresques – Valses romantiques – España – La Membrolle – La Sulamite	34
III. Gwendoline – Le Roi malgré lui – Souvenir de Munich – Habanera	47
IV. Joyeuse Marche – Songs – Briséis – Bourrée Fantasque – last years – death	58
In Memoriam: tributes from contemporary musicians	69
Unpublished Letters	83
The Art-Collector	99

Illustrations

Caricature of Chabrier, by Detaille   *frontispiece*

Between pages 28 and 29

Autour du piano, by Fantin-Latour

Chabrier, by Manet

Chabrier with the Wagnerian tenor Van Dyck

Chabrier (N*adar*)

The garden at La Membrolle (M. T. *Mabille*)

Lamoureux, Chabrier and Wilder

Excerpt from the manuscript score of *Jean Hunyade*

Autograph letter from Chabrier

Foreword

The conversational tone of this study may perhaps cause some lifted eyebrows amongst its readers, but I believe that it fits its subject, and even dare to hope that Chabrier himself would not have disapproved.

Long before I was able to judge his work from a technical point of view, as a young man I had been passionately attached to his music, at the same time so accessible and so elevated.

Having had to approach so many people who had known Chabrier intimately, I felt I was writing about a musical grandfather. That is why I have sometimes allowed myself the use of the first person, unusual in this kind of monograph, to give more immediacy and warmth, with the aim of making this highly significant composer as much *loved* as *admired*.

As a pupil of Ricardo Viñes, one of Chabrier's first interpreters, I feel permitted to give some brief technical suggestions to pianists, who are often worried by a very idiosyncratic style which is not as easy-going as it seems.

Finally, I hope that I may be able to convince both experts and laymen that, together with Fauré, Debussy, Ravel and Satie, Chabrier represents whatever is best in French music since 1880.

F.P.

[A few elucidatory footnotes necessary to the English edition have been added by the translator. These are marked—(Trans.).]

A Portrait of Chabrier

A PORTRAIT OF CHABRIER

> Chabrier, merry as a lark
> And melodious as a nightingale
> > P. VERLAINE

There are plenty of representations of Chabrier (photographs, caricatures, busts, and portraits), not to mention two beautiful paintings by Manet, but no less an authority than Messager considered that Chabrier's essence—a mixture of good-natured roguery—was exactly caught by Fantin-Latour's famous picture *Autour du piano*, now in the Louvre.

A strong, round head with a fleshy, sensual nose, prominent eyes, short arms, chubby hands, short legs: these were Chabrier's chief characteristics, typical of the Auvergne, dare I say those of a genuine *bougnat*.[1] Chabrier never denied his mountain origins: he used to say jokingly: "They're all ugly where I come from, capable at most of being water-carriers or wits . . . I know which I am."

His wit had in fact the effect of transforming this slightly awkward provincial into a highly urbane creature. It happens to many artists coming from distant parts of France. Could anyone be more Parisian than Mauriac (from Bordeaux) or Georges Auric, born at Lodève (in Provence)?

But let us return to the picture by Fantin-Latour. Detaille's famous caricature (*see frontispiece*) shows Chabrier back-view, and dishevelled, at the piano; his top-hat awry, and his famous mustard-coloured raglan coat draped round him like a dressing-gown. The Louvre picture, on the other hand, shows him

[1] *bougnat* = the peasant type who has left his native heath to go to the capital (Trans.).

Emmanuel Chabrier

as carefully dressed as the perfect office boss. In fact, most of his pictures show him in the guise of *fonctionnaire*.

Like Cézanne and Manet, Chabrier belonged to the middle-class innovators, so typical of the second half of the nineteenth century. A son and grandson of lawyers, he always remained a "gentleman" in spite of his eccentric side: his native Ambert dubbed all original and imaginative people as *foutraud* (devil-may-care) without seeing any harm in it. There is no better proof of Chabrier's bourgeois ideals than this surprising letter, congratulating his friend the tenor Van Dyck on his engagement to Mlle Servais.

> La Membrolle, Saturday morning [1886]
>
> Your letter has just come. We are bewildered and delighted. Joy and astonishment mixed. *Lugete, Veneres, Cupidinesque*. The Van Dyck of the salons, Ernest of the boudoirs, the rolling eye, the attested darling of Anglo-Franco-Belgian ladies, will soon cease to exist. He has become a Knight of the Grail, soon he will enter some fine cathedral, and kneeling before the altar of God, a serious "yes" will escape his lips. And now go bald, there is nothing to stop you: bid an eternal farewell to the world, to the *demi-monde*: have children, like me: love your life, as I love mine, and again like me, love this imbecile, music. Servais warm. Servais hot. Will it take place in August? Then Servais boiling hot.

Let us return once more to the picture by Fantin.

Nowadays one might think it was a *hommage à Chabrier*. But nothing of the kind, since in spite of the fame of *España*, Chabrier in 1884 was still considered an amateur. Most critics and music-lovers considered that the great composer of the group was Vincent d'Indy, the handsome young man to the right of the picture. The score of *Le Roi malgré lui* (which I am lucky enough to possess) bears the dedication:

A Portrait of Chabrier

"To my dear Vincent (d'Indy for posterity)."

But sometimes posterity plays the tease, and amateurs outwit professionals—as did Mussorgsky with Rimsky-Korsakov.

So if Chabrier is at the centre of Fantin's painting, it is only because he was the pianist of the group. He is known to have played the piano with astonishing fiery abandon: lacking a piano, he was a fish out of water, as can be seen in this extract from a letter to his parents:

Amsterdam, 1865

Six days, and I haven't touched a piano. I'm all of an itch, and take to playing on my hat, on the table in front of me, on my neighbour's back, or anywhere else handy.

In his *Profils de musiciens*, Hugues Imbert also mentions a strange organ in Chabrier's music-room. What follows is Imbert's own picturesque description of one of those magical *soirées* in the rue Mosnier.

There was Saint-Saëns, with his Parisian sense of fun and prodigious musical memory; Massenet, looking like a repentant Mary Magdalen . . . Manet, leader of the Impressionists, and many others I have since forgotten. Saint-Saëns sang and acted the part of Marguerite in Gounod's *Faust* with passionate ardour. And what accompaniments, what a formidable orchestra! Among other instruments there was a remarkable organ, capable of the most bizarre imitations: the boom of cannon, drums, etc. It was springtime, and the windows of the little mezzanine of rue Mosnier were wide open, so that passers-by used to crowd to listen to melodies which darted away at a first hearing.

In two celebrated paintings, *La rue Mosnier aux paveurs* (Road-menders in rue Mosnier) and *La rue Mosnier aux drapeaux* (Flags in rue Mosnier) Manet has represented the actual beflagged street where Chabrier lived at No. 23.

Emmanuel Chabrier

After his marriage to Alice Dejean, daughter of a well-known architect, on 27 December, 1873, Chabrier settled in Montmartre, where he remained for the rest of his life. He lived first in rue Mosnier, then in rue Rochechouart, and finally in avenue Trudaine, where he died.

The atmosphere of Montmartre was exactly right for a night wanderer, a lover of life in every shape and form. Naturally Montmartre at that period was not like the Montmartre of today, full of strip-tease clubs. Almost all the Impressionist painters lived there, and painted its most poetic aspects.

The crew of the "Bateau lavoir" (or "Scullery Ship"), with Picasso at their head, dealt a death-blow to the artistic prestige of La Butte[1] by transferring themselves to Montparnasse. All the same, I often visited Braque in Montmartre in 1923 in his studio in rue Caulaincourt, and my dear friend Max Jacob in rue Gabrielle. In the 'eighties, Montmartre was swarming with life in just the way that Chabrier loved—and how fond he also was of the Opéra district and the Grands Boulevards.

Crossing the Seine at that time implied a major expedition; the place du Théâtre Français was the limit of residential Paris. When Chabrier set out to visit "le père Franck", in the heart of the left bank, he felt he was off to the provinces. It is also true to say that in a period when Cézanne was anxious to exhibit at Le Bouguereau, and Mallarmé wrote his *Hérodiade* for performance in the Théâtre Français, the state-subsidized undertakings represented not mere official recognition, but recognition, full stop.

Heaven knows whether Chabrier was proud of having *Gwendoline* mounted at the Opéra, and *Le Roi malgré lui* at the Opéra-Comique. Avant-garde snobbery did not exist for him, and he felt himself well-placed—considering their respective value—between Saint-Saëns and Paul Vidal. Chabrier was the very embodiment of anti-snobbery.

In this he can justly be compared with Colette, who used

[1] The name given to the hill of Montmartre (Trans.).

A Portrait of Chabrier

to allow some of her most beautiful works to appear for the first time in *La Vie Parisienne*. There is no doubt that if Chabrier had been asked to insert *L'Île heureuse* as a musical supplement in a number of *Sourire*, he would have accepted, and how wise he would have been!

This did not stop him from preferring Manet to Meissonier. Is it commonly realized that the famous *Bar aux Folies-Bergère* hung above his piano? Chabrier had a real passion for painting, and when after his death his collection was disposed of at the Hôtel des Ventes on 26 March, 1896, it was found to contain some of the greatest masterpieces of the French School: Cézanne's *Harvesters*, the *Bar aux Folies-Bergère*, Manet's *Skating* and *The Hare*, Renoir's *Leaving the Conservatoire*, seven Monets and two Sisleys. This gives the lie to those who limit his art to the marvellous posters of Chéret. As solidly based in mind as in body, this "Auvergnat" found it perfectly possible to reconcile friendship with Manet and with Detaille, creator of the ravishing *Rêve*.

In the field of music, he was as friendly with Fauré and d'Indy as with Lecocq, Messager and Paul Lacôme, composer of the celebrated *Estudiantina*, which used to be churned out by all the big steam roundabouts at the Trône Fair.

In the literary field, although he had been Verlaine's friend from the age of 19, Chabrier showed such eclectic tastes that he became, alas, a lifelong slave of the incorrigible Catulle Mendès. This man held forth at the Café Napolitain, where Chabrier would often join him after the theatre.

I have never been fully able to understand this question of Mendès. One has only to read the libretto of Messager's *Isoline* to realize what kind of writer he was. One day in Colette's presence I expressed astonishment at the prestige this mountebank enjoyed in the 1880s. With marvellous peasant logic, Colette replied: "What do you expect, he was a Zeus, smelling of patchouli!"[1]

[1] Used before the era of moth-balls! (Trans.).

Later I will come back to Mendès' pernicious influence on Chabrier, but at this stage I only want to place a character who so often falsified Chabrier's aesthetic sense in operatic matters: a composer who was much more capable of writing an opera on Rabelais—as he sometimes planned—than to play the Wagnerian, as he did in *Gwendoline*. It is all the more strange as a collaboration in that Chabrier was just as sure of himself in literature as in painting. "I am the least illiterate of composers," he would say. And it was true: his astonishing correspondence shows it.

Some of his letters might have been written by Colette herself. Here are some lines addressed to his old Nanine, the nurse who had brought him up:

> La Membrolle, Monday, 31 March, 1890
> My little Nanine,
> No news from the country: nobody's passed out, they're all holding on. I caught a glimpse of the cow-girl, who is letting her moustache grow: she's still not married.

And in another to Nanine:

> On Sunday there was a big procession, street altars and the children's first communion: everybody has requisitioned flowers and flowering branches, all the green and pink of the village.

From Holland he wrote to his parents:

> At Scheveningen, where I went twice, the ladies behave better than last year. Every so often there's a little bareness, a torso visible at long distances: but the sea is always rough, and cuts one's admiration in two: a wave, poof, and you can't see any more.

Where humour was concerned, Chabrier was unrivalled. Of the composer of *Mignon*, he wrote: "There are three kinds of music: good, bad, and that of Ambroise Thomas." When

Benjamin Godard whispered: "What a pity, my dear Emmanuel, that you took to music so late," Chabrier replied simply: "It's much more annoying, my dear Benjamin, that you took to it so early."

Sometimes his language was disconcertingly earthy. Princesse Edmond de Polignac has vouched to me for the truth of the following anecdote: some days after the first private hearing of *Gwendoline*, she gave a dinner for Chabrier in her studio (she was then Princesse de Scey-Montbéliard). When the asparagus appeared, Chabrier leant towards her, and said: "Do help yourself, Madame, but it makes dreadful urine!"

No description of Chabrier would be complete without a mention of his extraordinary sense of friendship and profound goodness of heart. Both are reflected in the marvellous letters signed "Ton Mavel" which he sent to his old Nanine from La Membrolle, Indre-et-Loire, when she was away ill. What a charming letter to distract an invalid!:

La Membrolle, 16 May, 1890

... I can't send you any flowers or fruit, nothing's out yet. Probably Nature is getting ready for her big outburst of roses—at present only buds are to be seen—and cherry-blossom; as soon as the strawberries "yield", as they say, and we catch sight of the first cherries, we'll send you a nice little basketful.

Chabrier was always one to help, tender as a husband, vigilant as a father, and a model son-in-law, at a time when mothers-in-law were figures of fun. The following incident is typical of him.

In 1892, Adolphe Sax, inventor of the saxophone, was declared a bankrupt at the age of 78, and so stripped of the Order of the Légion d'honneur. Paul Lacôme and Chabrier jointly organized an appeal to rehabilitate a man without whom jazz would certainly never have existed. Although Chabrier was already very ill (he died two years later, in 1894), he busied himself frantically in the cause, writing around to everyone, and making personal representations. But, unfortunately, all to no avail.

Vincent d'Indy nicknamed him the "Angel of Drollery". Droll, certainly, to the point of genius, but all of it rarefied by a generous heart, which spent itself to its last gasp for those he loved, and for his beloved music.

Life and Work

I

CHILDHOOD
YEARS OF APPRENTICESHIP
L'ÉTOILE – L'EDUCATION MANQUÉE

Emmanuel Chabrier was born on 18 January, 1841, at Ambert (Puy-de-Dôme). Those who know Ambert's delicious cheese will not be surprised that he was proverbially known as a gourmand.

His father, Jean Chabrier, was a lawyer. The family had been settled in Ambert since the eighteenth century, and had provided the town with merchants, priests and lawyers. His mother, Marie-Anne-Evelina Durozay, came from Cusset-Vichy, in nearby Bourbonnais.

Chabrier inherited his father's thick-set shoulders and his mother's refinement of spirit. An only son, his childhood was spent at Ambert until the age of twelve.

At six he began studying the piano with M. Saporta, a Spanish Carlist refugee, but his parents attached no importance to this middle-class ritual. Yet because his mother sang, and apparently had a charming voice, the little boy was set to learn the instrument. Once, when a friend of his parents began to play the piano, the young boy amazed the guests with his wild excitement. I know that that is the sort of anecdote often invented by posterity, but it is a fact that in three years of study he showed such progress that he was able to play a concerto under a conductor whose name has unfortunately been lost.

According to Messager, Chabrier did not have particularly pianistic hands, as they were small and round, with short wrists; but the demon of piano-playing was so strong in him that he drew sparks from the keyboard.

Anxious about his schooling (certainly not his music lessons), his father moved in 1853 to Clermont-Ferrand, where Emmanuel became a pupil at the Lycée Blaise Pascal. There he took violin lessons with a man called Tarnovski. So dazzled was this teacher by his talent that he suggested to his father he should make a virtuoso of him. Jean Chabrier was shocked at the idea of his son taking up such a perilous career, and declared point-blank that music would never be more for Emmanuel than a pastime. More advisedly, Mme Chabrier let the lessons continue their regular course.

In any case, the child made such good progress that his father soon thought of an ideal occupation for him: a post at the Ministry of the Interior! Accordingly, in 1856 the family left Clermont-Ferrand, and settled in Paris (No. 23, then No. 40, rue Vaneau).

Chabrier obtained his *baccalauréat* on 4 November, 1858, and in 1861 took his degree in Law. To his father's great delight, he entered the Ministry on 29 October, 1863, as a forwarding clerk in the so-called Copying Bureau!

Confronted by his son's university successes, Jean Chabrier finally let the reins lie loosely. The young Emmanuel set out to conquer Paris.

He was well enough off to be able to continue his musical studies as he wished. He became a piano pupil of Edouard Wolf, and a composer-violinist, Richard Hommer, who had been an old friend of Chopin. Soon he began a frenzied study of fugue and counterpoint, first with Semet, erstwhile winner of the Prix de Rome, and more particularly with Aristide Higuard, composer of *Hamlet*, an opera in five acts, which many considered better than that of Ambroise Thomas. He was certainly a good influence on Chabrier. Chabrier was still studying with him when he began working at the Ministry. He was then twenty-eight, and already knew many artists. It seems that Verlaine was one of his first companions, because in his copy of *Jadis et Naguère* (1891 ed.) Chabrier wrote: "For two or three years, from 1860-1863, I went almost every Saturday to dine at the house of Mme Verlaine in rue Lecluze, near the boulevard des Batignolles."

Verlaine has left a gentle re-evocation of the memory of those evenings in his sonnet to Emmanuel Chabrier, published in *Amour*:

> Chabrier, nous faisions, un ami cher et moi,
> Des paroles pour vous qui leur donniez des ailes,
> Et tous trois frémissions quand, pour bénir nos zèles,
> Passait l'*Ecce Deus* et le je ne sais quoi.
>
> Chez ma mère charmante et divinement bonne
> Votre génie improvisait au piano.
> Et c'était tout autour comme un brûlant anneau
> De sympathie et d'aise qui rayonne.
>
> Hélas ma mère est morte et l'ami cher est mort
> Et me voilà semblable au chrétien près du port,
> Qui surveille les tout derniers écueils du monde.
>
> Non toutefois sans saluer à l'horizon
> Comme une voile sur le large un blanc frisson
> Le souvenir des frais instants de paix profonde.

[Chabrier, we used to fashion, a dear friend and I, words for you who gave them wings, and we all three trembled when, to bless our efforts, came the *Ecce Deus* and that which I cannot describe.

At the house of my charming and divinely good mother your genius would improvise at the piano; and it was as though all around us shone a glowing ring of fellowship and ease.

Alas, my mother is dead, and the dear friend is dead, and

here I am like the Christian nearing his haven who looks on the very last reefs of this world. Not, however, without saluting on the horizon a flutter of white like a sail on the open sea: the memory of those fresh moments of profound peace.]

The "dear friend" was Lucien Viotti, who with Verlaine was co-author of Chabrier's first operetta libretti: *Fisch-Ton-Kan* (1863) and *Vaucochard et fils Ier* (1864).

From the moment of arrival in Paris, Chabrier was unable to resist the lure of the bookshop of the publisher Lemerre. His ground-floor rooms still exist in ghost-fashion in passage Choiseul. This was the meeting-place of the Parnassians: Richepin, Heredia, Coppée and Mendès.

Chabrier first came to know Villiers de l'Isle d'Adam—himself a remarkably gifted musician—at the house of the Marquise de Ricard. The dedication of the *Contes cruels* bears witness to his teaching:

To my friend Emmanuel Chabrier from his well-intentioned musical apprentice, with heartfelt admiration
VILLIERS DE L'ISLE-ADAM.

Another of Chabrier's favourite haunts was the astonishing salon of Ninna de Callas, frequented by all the young intellectuals of the day. It was there that he met Manet.

Amongst the composers whom Chabrier mixed with at this time were Fauré, d'Indy and Saint-Saëns, his contemporaries: Lalo and Reyer, his seniors: Duparc, Bordes and Chausson, his juniors. "Le Père Franck" he saw rarely, but always with great respect.

I have always wondered why he never mentions Bizet in his correspondence, and Gounod very seldom. Since Chabrier was 34 at the time of the first performance of *Carmen* (1875), and *Faust* dates from 1860, was it possible for a well-educated young man, newly arrived in Paris, to remain indifferent? As

Life and Work

he only came to be aware of Wagner in 1879, it is strange that he should have failed to recognize such masterpieces. If Chabrier had only learned from Bizet, and instead of Mendès' ineptitudes had found a libretto like that of *Carmen*, what a masterpiece he might have given us! As for Gounod, I am certain that it is from him that consciously or unconsciously Chabrier derived his melodic sense. Ravel with his marvellous professional skill hit the nail on the head when he chose Siebel's aria (*Faites-lui mes aveux*) as the theme for his *A la manière de Chabrier*. In his hands the theme becomes more typical of Chabrier than if it had been written by Chabrier himself. Take for example these few bars:

Few of Chabrier's works from 1860 to 1877 need to hold our attention, apart from a ravishing *Impromptu* for piano (1872), dedicated to Mme Manet, and first performed by Saint-Saëns at the Societé Nationale on 27 January, 1877. Earlier on, there is also the *Marche des Cipayes*, anticipating the *Joyeuse Marche* of 1888, but not very much else.

Some unpublished fragments of his first two operettas—*Fisch-Ton-Kan* and *Vaucochard et Fils Ier*—were written in collaboration with Verlaine and Viotti, and date from the years 1863-1864. These fragments have only once been given

Emmanuel Chabrier

in public, by courtesy of Mme Bretton-Chabrier, in the Salle du Conservatoire, on 22 April, 1941. I had the honour of playing the piano part in *Fisch-Ton-Kan* and Roger Désormière, a convinced Chabrian, conducted *Vaucochard*.

Authentic Chabrier was already clearly discernible in these operetta fragments, particularly in the *Chanson de l'homme armé*, which from the point of view of text-setting is full of pleasant surprises—but quite minor by comparison with *L'Étoile*.

In 1867, Chabrier had the curious idea of asking Henri Fouquier for an opera based on the history of the Hunyadi. I am not quite clear what Hungary had in common with Chabrier's style. Fouquier drew up a libretto in two acts, on which Chabrier worked for some time. Although he discarded it, *Jean Hunyade* contained some very beautiful things.

I think that Chabrier showed himself too critical of this work, unless he could not stomach the libretto, which was only too understandable. I have been able to make a very careful study of the orchestral score, by courtesy of the heirs of Mme Bretton-Chabrier. The following comments appear on the cover of a manuscript of Italian format:

"It's a little faded [note of 1892]: when Marcel [Chabrier's son] looks at this manuscript in 1920, it will be a great deal more so." And later on: "Ah! this does not belong to yesterday. Even in 1892, Fouquier always cuts an elegant figure, but at this period [1867], turning the corner of rue de Berri on the Champs-Elysées, he was devilishly more stylish than he is now." And lastly, this significant comment: "This music contains two leitmotivs which were used in *Gwendoline* and in *Briseïs*." The themes are subsequently underlined in the manuscript.

The four numbers of which it is comprised are naturally unequal, but contain many anticipations of the later Chabrier. The whole of the beginning is orchestrated for wind. The

Autour du piano, *by Fantin-Latour*

Chabrier, by Manet

Chabrier with the Wagnerian tenor Van Dyck

Chabrier (Nadar)

The garden at La Membrolle (M. T. Mabille)

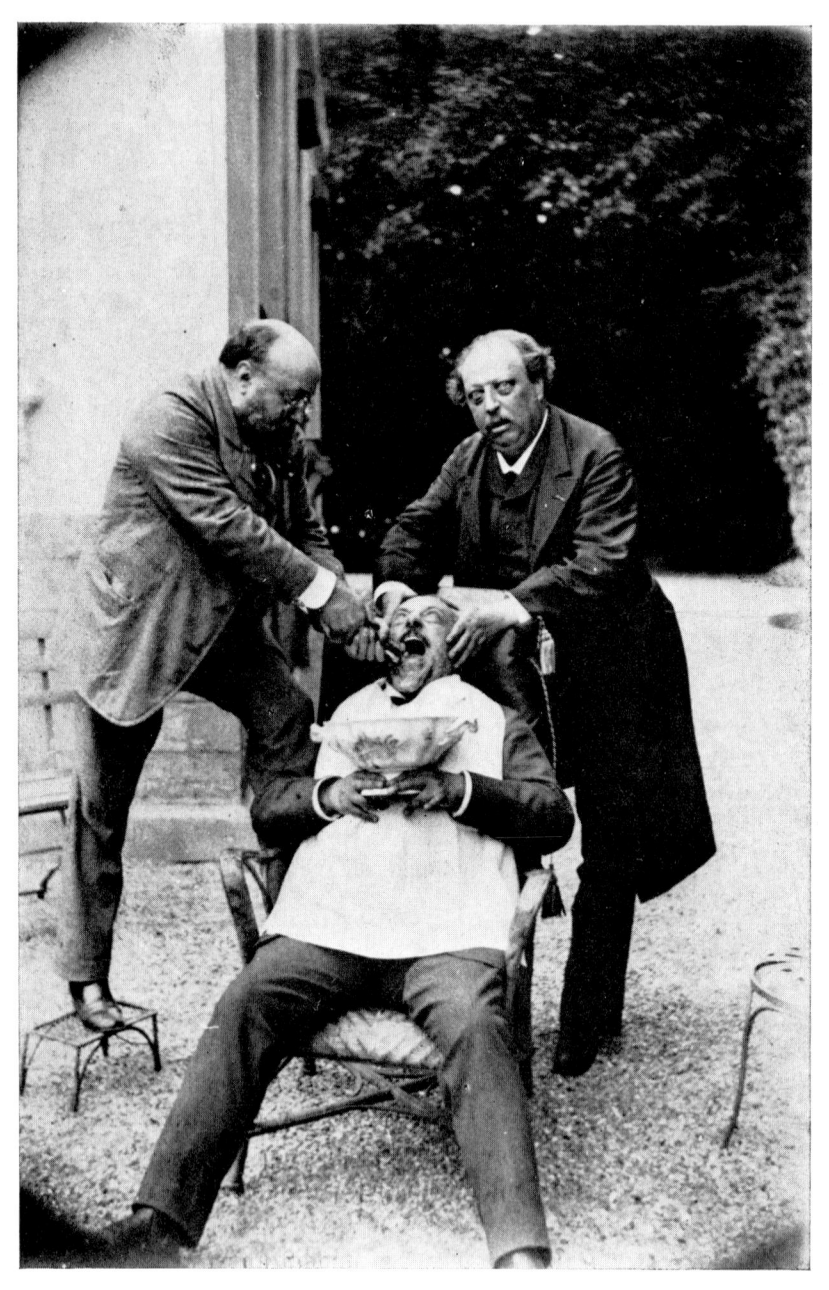

Lamoureux, Chabrier and Wilder

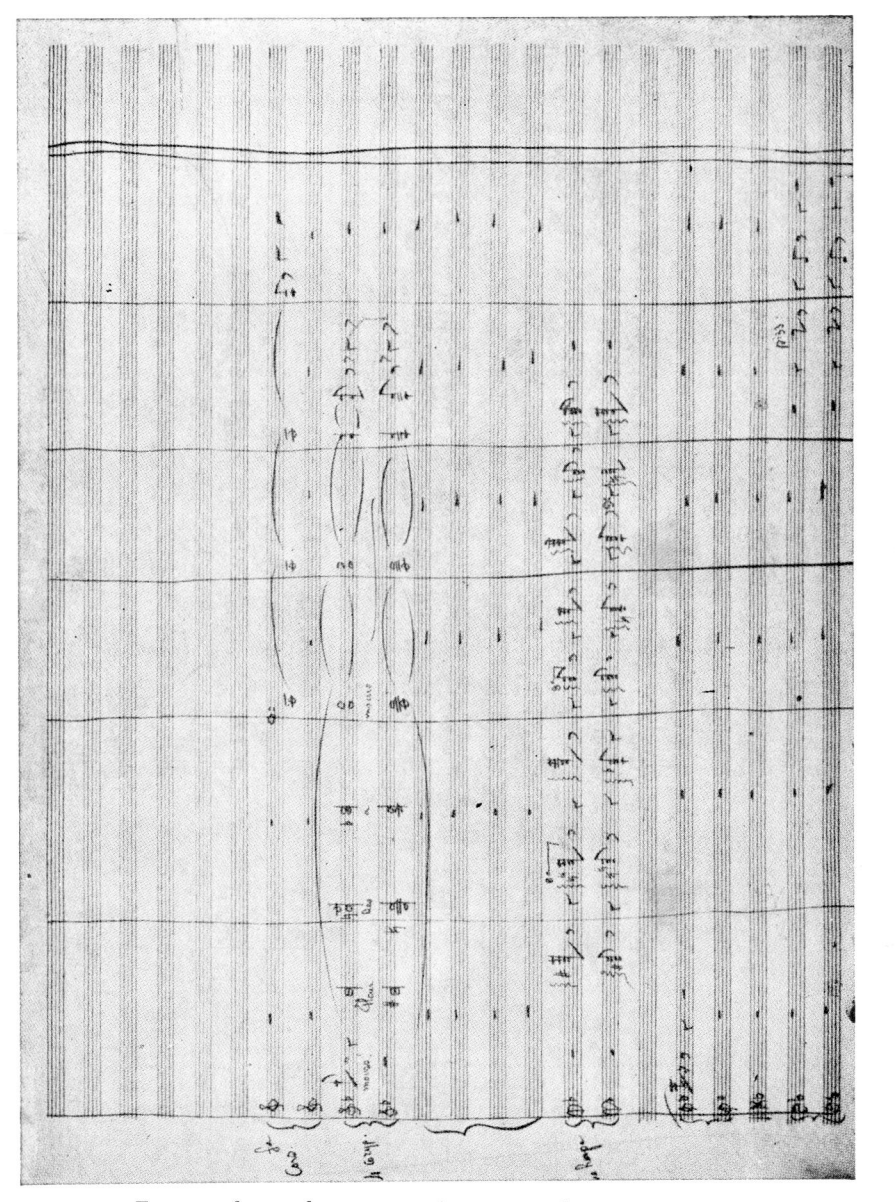

Excerpt from the manuscript score of Jean Hunyade

BAINS D'OSTENDE — KURSAAL

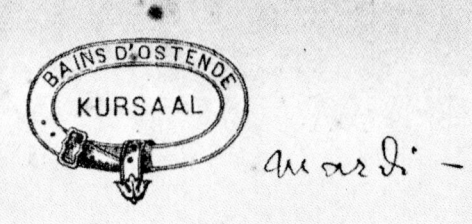

Mardi —

Nous revenons demain et serons à la gare par le train de 3h½ ou de 6h 05. — Temps superbe. J'ai dirigé España au Kursaal et l'on m'a fait une ovation. Nous nous amusons comme des fous.

À demain
v,t,
Emmanuel

Autograph letter from Chabrier

strings only enter after ten pages. Some of the instrumental combinations already show an astonishing freedom.

As a specimen of Chabrier's musical script, I have deliberately chosen the end of a chorus from *Jean Hunyade* because of its entrancing lay-out, as simple as it is ingenious. Some syncopated chords for the harp accompany four female members of the chorus, and at the end a low sustained note from the horn blots out the light female voices in an unexpected way.

Perhaps one day this unpublished work will be given a hearing? I firmly believe so, but present the above as a reference!

To complete this rapid survey of Chabrier's work from 1860 to 1877, I must still mention a *Larghetto*, not all that interesting, for horn and orchestra. Such a small output may seem surprising. Indeed, Chabrier did not begin to compose intensively until the age of 35, and all his works were written in a comparatively short space of time, as he was 50 when he finished his last composition—the single act of his opera *Briseïs*. This does not mean that he should be accused of laziness. His greatest excuse was the laborious office job which he kept on until 1880. And then, as the saying went: "he had to sow his wild oats".

In 1873, Chabrier married Mlle Dejean, and so began a settled existence. In 1869, within eight days, he had lost both his father and mother. Since then he had lived alone with his faithful Nanine, who had never left him. Naturally she was incorporated into the young couple's life, which—thanks to her—experienced no domestic worries. Some years later two boys were born, Marcel and André, who gave their father much joy.

In this family atmosphere, Chabrier began composing regularly. In 1877 a chance opportunity led to his first success. Two famous librettists, Leterrier and Vanlo, who had already collaborated with Lecocq (*Giroflé-Girofla*, 1874, and

La Petite Mariée, 1875) were looking for a young composer to set a curious libretto called *L'Étoile*.

Leterrier and Vanlo met Chabrier at Hirsch's house, when he played them some songs and piano pieces. They were at once enchanted by so much invention and fantasy, and suggested working together. Chabrier accepted, and immediately set to work. In a few months the score was finished, but knowing little of theatrical requirements, he made no piano transcription, assuming that rehearsals always took place with orchestra. No matter! For three weeks, Chabrier became a rehearsal pianist. And what a pianist!

The first performance took place on 28 November, 1877, at the Bouffes-Parisiens. The libretto of *L'Étoile* is so complicated that it seems useless to describe it here. The music is so strongly defined, alert and lively that there is not a dull moment in the whole three acts, in spite of the mediocre text. As a great admirer of Offenbach, Chabrier took to imitating him directly in some details of his prosody. Hence *Donnez-vous la peine de vous asseoir* (chanson du pal) is directly derived from *Roi barbu qui s'avance, bu qui s'avance* in *La belle Hélène*:

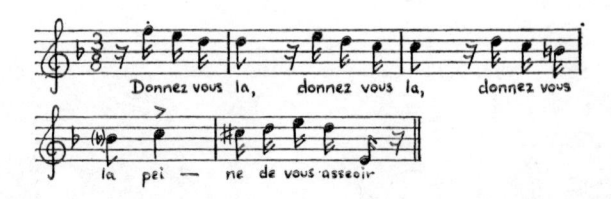

But while Offenbach's music reminds one of frothy champagne, Chabrier, in spite of his verve, is often much more tender and full of feeling. Typical examples are the *Romance à l'Étoile*, the adorable "Swooning Scene" and the Rose couplets. Confronted by such charm, how could one resist the lively "Hawkers' Rondo", set in the comic style of Frère Jacques, the quartet of the employees, the *Air du pal*, and above all the entrancing duet *de la chartreuse verte,* a sort of parody on an *arietta* by Donizetti?

Apparently Debussy split his sides with laughter when he heard this duet. *L'Étoile* was a resounding success in a very careful staging, with settings by Grévin and Robida, and an excellent cast, headed by Daubray and Paola Marié. The critics were unanimous in its praise, and the whole musical world, one might say, came to applaud the masterpiece. For the first time, Chabrier stopped being treated as a gifted amateur.

Everything promised well, but alas, as always in his theatrical career, Chabrier was the victim of misfortune; after 48 performances, the piece disappeared from the boards. The excuse given was that one of the performers was ill, but—as M. René Martineau suggests in his excellent book *Chabrier*—it seems likely that the cause was a contract between the authors and the theatre, according to which the management took on much greater responsibility after the fiftieth performance . . . Since that time *L'Étoile* has only had occasional performances. It was last seen in 1941, when Jacques Rouché mounted it at the Opéra-Comique under the conductor Roger Désormière. It was given entrancing sets by Dignimont, and a skilfully revised libretto ought to have ensured a lasting success. Unfortunately, the period was not one for laughter . . .

Quite apart from its intrinsic qualities, *L'Étoile* is the source of subsequent French operetta, particularly that of Messager. For the first time, Chabrier introduced into *opéra bouffe* a careful attention to harmony and orchestration, which had previously been missing, except in Offenbach and Lecocq. I myself thought much about *L'Étoile* while I was writing *Les Mamelles de Tirésias.*

In 1877, Chabrier sketched out a one-act comic opera called *Le Sabbat,* using a libretto by Armand Silvestre, but he soon gave it up. I am forced to agree with him, having read the libretto, which is incredibly vacuous.

Emmanuel Chabrier

Round about 1878, he composed two comic duets intended for a team who sang in the salons, Bruat-Rivière, but they never sang them. From what I know of *Cocodette et Cocorico* and *Monsieur et Madame Orchestre*, they are no more than good-natured sketches.

On 1 May, 1879, at the Cercle de la Presse, Chabrier came up with a new masterpiece called *L'Éducation manquée*, which earned him a success equal to that of *L'Étoile*. The librettists of this little one-act theatre-piece were Leterrier and Vanlo. How are we to describe the plot? The young Gontran de Boimassif, on the eve of his wedding to Hélène de la Cerisaie, finds himself greatly embarrassed as to how to . . . fulfil his marital function. Master Pausanias has taught him many subjects, "mythology, metallurgy, agronomy, heliography, orthopaedy, etc." but has never so much as mentioned the subject. Gontran imperiously summons Pausanias, and orders him to discover as quickly as possible a way of overcoming such a very curious fear.

No sooner has Pausanias turned his back when happily a violent storm breaks out. Gontran, holding a terrified Hélène in his arms, soon discovers the way to marital bliss.

This is a simple enough trifle, but Chabrier's genius polishes up the libretto in the purest "Louis XV bonbon box" style. Each page of this piece shows the hand of the master. The orchestration, which is very sparse, has a delicious ring to it. Everything deserves to be quoted: Pausanias' drinking song, his comic aria on his ideas of teaching, the *Sicilienne* before the storm, and the final duet with its *Envoi* to the public.

Travesti roles were all the rage at this time, so the charming Jane Hading took the part of Gontran, just as the Hawker in *L'Étoile* had been taken by Paola Marié. Jane Hading was a comedy actress, not a real singer. Stylistically, *L'Éducation* did not call for a big voice, but an interpreter who could do justice to this kind of dolt. Hading succeeded admirably.

The poverty of the spoken text has often impeded the pro-

Life and Work

gress of *L'Education*. In 1934, Diaghilev asked Darius Milhaud to compose some recitatives. In my opinion, this is the only version which does the work justice. The high quality of Diaghilev's production was set off by a set and costumes by Juan Gris.

II

THE WAGNER SHOCK – *PIECES PITTORESQUES* – *VALSES ROMANTIQUES* – *ESPAÑA* – *LA MEMBROLLE* – *LA SULAMITE*

On Monday, 7 July, 1879, Chabrier wrote to Paul Lacôme from Cauteret:

> I'm not feeling at all well: I'm worried about an eye and an ear, both on the same side. Perhaps something's the matter with me?

This may well have been one of the first signs of the paralysis which was to silence him fifteen years later, but it did not prevent him from leaving for Munich some few weeks later to attend a performance of *Tristan*. In this connection, I would like to quote the wonderful letter he wrote to his office chief, M. Gustave Desjardins:

[1879]

> As private business matters oblige me to leave for Bordeaux, I would be most grateful if you would permit me the three days' leave which are needed for their discussion.
>
> The above is for the office record: but because I have never lied, which may perhaps be why I have always enjoyed the sympathetic respect of my superiors, I owe you the true version, as follows: I am not going to Bordeaux at all. For as long as ten years—and you can imagine how it has grown in this time—I have been possessed by a longing to see Wagner's *Tristan und Isolde*. It can only be seen in Germany, and it is being played on Sunday in Munich.

I could resist no longer, and today I went to Avricourt—now our frontier, alas—to get a visa. I was successful.

That is my crime, Monsieur mon chef. I beg you to pardon this flight from administrative duty, and to trust my conscientiousness. On Wednesday morning at the latest I shall be back at the office.

I am, Sir,
Your most obedient Servant,
EM. CHABRIER.

It was lucky that M. Desjardins granted the necessary permission, because this journey altered Chabrier's destiny. A very charming letter from Henri Duparc to René Martineau, dated 15 January, 1908, gives valuable details about this journey:

... some superb performances of *Tristan und Isolde* were being given in Munich, and I went to hear the première, on a Sunday. I was so excited that I came back to Paris to persuade some friends of mine to come and hear the second performance, due to take place the following Sunday. One of these friends was Chabrier, whom I found at his Ministry: he hesitated for a long time, and put many difficulties in the way; but it seems that I succeeded in persuading him, because he ended up by promising to come with us. Everyone was glad of it, because it ensured us an amusing journey. He was the victim of such strong emotion that in spite of his natural gaiety, he left us after the performance to shut himself up in his room. At that time, as you know, he was not intending to commit himself entirely to music; *Tristan* showed him where his vocation lay. When he came back from Munich, his mind was made up.

In fact, in 1880, shortly after his return, Chabrier decided to resign his post at the Ministry of the Interior. Clearly from a financial point of view it was a risky move, but all the same he could no longer compose music as an amateur. Moreover, he was always being attacked on this score. Nowadays, the Conservatoire, the Prix de Rome, and other academic honours scarcely matter, but at that time it was quite different. How often did Saint-Saëns or Massenet feel they had to let Chabrier know he was not one of them! Fully convinced of his mission, he wanted at all costs to put a stop to this.

I do not agree with Alfred Cortot when he writes in his book *Musique française de piano*:

> Coming late to music, at least from a fully professional point of view, Chabrier was never fully independent as a composer: he never acquired the facility which comes, at least where composition is concerned, by regular discipline imposed at the right stage.

Chabrier's style never owed anything to anyone else, and though he might have acquired the knowledge of ready-made formulae had he been taught by a Théodore Dubois, his inventiveness and daring might have been impaired thereby. Though we may lament Wagner's influence on a composer who was French to the marrow of his bones (in any case the influence is less oppressive than commonly supposed), we have to bless this journey to Munich, from which Chabrier returned with renewed energies. "There is music in it for a hundred years; he's not left us a bone to pick. Who would dare? . . ."

Like most prophecies, this was rapidly contradicted by Chabrier himself, and by Fauré, Debussy and Ravel, who fled at full tilt from the Wagnerian credo. Berg made a similar error of judgement later on when he wrote that "serial music ensures the supremacy of German music for a hundred years". In fact, it is Boulez in France, and Dallapiccola, Petrassi, Nono, Maderna and Berio in Italy who have made the most of Schoenberg's influence.

It should also be emphasized that it was Wagner's genius for opera which influenced Chabrier, not his composing methods. Duparc's letter to René Martineau, quoted above, also informs us that Duparc had lent Chabrier a score from which to follow the performance, and that he had underlined countless passages—*all* of them passages of emotional intensity. In short, thanks to Wagner, Chabrier discovered his *élan vital*, but even in *Gwendoline* always stayed faithful to his radiant ideal.

The best proof is that two years after this journey to Munich he wrote his ten *Pièces pittoresques* for piano (1881), which deliberately turn their back on Wagner. Without hesitation I declare that the *Pièces pittoresques* are as important for French music as Debussy's *Préludes*.

At this time, neither Saint-Saëns nor Fauré had gone so far in their search for new sound textures. Not one of these ten pieces but shows the mark of complete originality. Alas, they are too seldom played: perhaps because nobody is quite sure how to play them.

Among true interpreters of Chabrier, I would mention Édouard Risler, Ricardo Viñes, Robert Casadesus and Marcelle Meyer.

In these pieces it is not so much a question of getting the better of technical problems—numerous though these are—but of finding the true style of the music, so admirably constructed in spite of its easy-going manner. The real solution is a mixture of strictness and relaxation. Moreover Chabrier has carefully marked what he wants—and *all his indications of tempo are exact*. As there is none given for the *Improvisation* and the *Scherzo valse*, I propose below markings which follow the Viñes tradition. Lastly—and most important—the composer has marked all the rubatos; free as it is of all coyness or affectation, the rest of the time this music needs to be played quite straight.

At the time these pieces were written, what was known as *"genre"* music was all the rage. It could be facile, as in Chaminade, or of transcendent difficulty, as in the concert

Emmanuel Chabrier

studies of Alkan, which were frequently performed by Diémer and Planté. Unlike d'Indy, who was attracted by sonata form, Chabrier found himself completely at home in such a free type of composition, which he entirely transcended.

Paysage is the first of the set, a joyous and not a romantic landscape, where living is meant to be enjoyed. This piece is generally played too slow because the indication *Allegro non troppo* (♩ = 132)—which is accurate—seems to be contradicted by the word *calme*. The piece needs playing with gaiety and tenderness.

Mélancolie is typical Chabrier, the type to which Ravel refers in his *A la manière de Chabrier*. Dare I suggest that these two exquisite pages should be played without the hands being entirely synchronized? This will shock some people, and my little book will be in danger of being burnt in the courtyard of the Conservatoire—but no matter, I take full responsibility! The great pianists of an earlier period—Planté, Paderewski, Sauer, etc.—did not *always* use strict synchronization. In any case, it seems quite as legitimate a means of expression as the *portamenti* or chest-notes used by singers!

In their ballet *Cotillon*, Christian Bérard and Balanchine turned *Tourbillon* into a typical salon *galop* of the 1880's, thereby showing real understanding of Chabrier. This piece must be played *implacably*.

Sous-bois: how often Ravel used to talk to me ecstatically about it! For him it was one of the high-water marks of Chabrier's work. Evidently, the extreme subtlety of its harmony, set on a steady rocking semi-quaver rhythm, held a fascination for the composer of *Oiseaux tristes*. *Sous-bois* should be played very evenly.

As for *Mauresque*, No. 5 of the set, Ravel's admiration took more concrete form, since in the *Forlane* of *Le Tombeau de Couperin* one can hear a slight echo of the middle section of this piece, a piece which needs playing in strict rhythm.

I lost my heart to *Idylle* when I first heard it in February,

1914. At that time *Petrouchka, Le Sacre* and the Six Piano Pieces of Schoenberg were lying on my piano: for all that I loved him, I foolishly believed, like many people even today, that Chabrier was a minor composer. One day I went by chance into a recording studio of Maison Pathé—opposite the Crédit Lyonnais in the Boulevard des Italiens—and from admiration for Risler inserted a coin into the automatic machine and dialled the number of *Idylle*. Even today it makes me tremble with emotion to think of the resultant miracle; a whole universe of harmony suddenly opened up before me, and my music has never forgotten that first kiss. A single work may well serve as a starting-point—Matisse's painting would never have become what it did without Cézanne's *Overture to Tannhäuser*.

Idylle requires delicate interpretation. It is essential not to turn midday into two o'clock! Set out at the exact speed indicated, and then go straight through the piece without the slightest rubato.

Danse Villageoise needs brisk playing. Above all do not slow down in the central section or the whole will become insipid.

Improvisation: rarely has Chabrier been as romantic as he is here. It needs playing at a very steady speed ($\decrescendo$ = c.60), like Liszt's *Rêve d'Amour*.

Now we come to the *Menuet pompeux* which is the master-key that unlocks many pages of Ravel and Debussy. It was orchestrated by Ravel in 1937, and the two versions of *Menuet antique*—the first for piano (1895), the second an orchestration—are so directly inspired by it that they are like reflections of Chabrier seen through a mirror. As for its influence on Debussy, I have often played these two bars of the *Menuet pompeux* to music-lovers who scorn Chabrier. and asked its source:

"Parbleu! that's Debussy," they cried. Yes, but a Debussy before his time, because the *Arabesques* date from 1888.

The *Scherzo valse* is often played too fast, so I feel it may be a good idea to give the real tempo, which is that of Viñes: (♩. = 192). This tempo, not too hurried, gives these famous pages their friskiness. The trio—where the crotchet is about equal to the earlier dotted crotchet, should be played in rustic fashion, and a little more heavily.

The first performance of the *Pièces pittoresques* was given by Mlle Marie Poitevin at the Société Nationale on 9th August, 1881.

It is worth noticing that the Société Nationale, founded in 1871 by Franck, Saint-Saëns, Castillon, Duparc and Chausson, always gave a warm welcome to Chabrier's works. He could have been one of its founding members, but we need to remember that in 1871 he was still considered an amateur.

It is a curious fact that the most intrepid pioneers have often been treated as amateurs. It was the case with Gesualdo, Mussorgsky, Satie. It may be because at the outset they were self-taught, and hence in no way the slaves of school rules, that they were all the more easily able to upset the barriers imposed by tradition.

There is no doubt that it was Chabrier's *instinctive* harmonic sense which made Camille Saint-Saëns take him for a Sunday composer, just as Rimsky corrected the audacities of *Boris Godunov*. Even today some people are moved to contest the harmonic relevance of the *Pièces pittoresques*. I have never believed it possible to demonstrate innovation with a pencil

Life and Work

in the hand, particularly when the composer is one to whom no rules apply. To say that some piece of music breaks new ground because it uses certain boldly juxtaposed intervals is too little, and too vague, where Chabrier is concerned. His interest lies in the unexpected choice of tonal groupings, and exists much more in the spirit than in the letter.

As Léon-Paul Fargue has neatly put it: "In Art we must first believe, and afterwards go and look". This is absolutely true of Chabrier. The fact that he guided Debussy, Ravel, and, after a lapse of time, the composers of my own generation, shows how fruitful were his discoveries.

In 1880, Chabrier had tried to write an opera on Claretie's *Les Muscadins*. He quickly gave up after four unfinished numbers. On one of them, a duet for two male voices, he wrote: "One of my most carefully composed pieces; d'Indy complimented me on it." It seems that as with *Jean Hunyade*, he was discouraged by the inadequacy of the libretto.

In 1882, Chabrier realized an old ambition, and spent the autumn in Spain. This stay in Andalusia was of great importance because it inspired *España*, the work which will ensure him a world reputation. I have always liked to think of this great visual piece having been evoked by a Spain seen through the paintings of Manet.

In ecstasy, Chabrier swamped his Parisian friends with fantastic letters. He wrote to his publishers, Enoch et Costallat, from Saint-Sébastien:

> The women are beautiful, the men well-made, and *señoras* with fine breasts often forget to do up their costumes on the beach; from now on I shall carry buttons and thread about with me. I have a passion for making myself useful.

From Seville:

> Well, my friends, now we can see Andalusian behinds wriggling about like delighted snakes.

Emmanuel Chabrier

From Granada (to Edouard Moullé):

> Since coming to Andalusia I haven't seen a really ugly woman: not to mention their feet, the smallest I've ever seen, their hands are tiny and well-groomed, and their arms of an exquisite shape: I won't let on what these women display, but they display it beautifully. Add to which the waves, the kiss-curls, and other ingenious devices of their hair-dressing, the inevitable fan, the flower in the chignon, the comb on one side, much in evidence, the floral shawl of crêpe-de-Chine, with its long tassels wrapped and knotted round their bodies: their arms bare and their eyelashes so long they could be curled, their complexions either matt white, or burnished golden, according to their race: they spend their time laughing, gesticulating, dancing, drinking, and a fig for Montceau-les-Mines.[1]

Chabrier himself had never mocked at Montmartre, and it was what Satie described as his "Piazza Clichy manner" which made *España* unintelligible to Spaniards.

Arbos tried to play *España* several times in Madrid, but with no success. *Rhapsodie espagnole* and *Ibéria* enjoy success in Spain because Ravel and Debussy evoke an atmosphere, whereas *España* for Spaniards is nothing but a poor relation of their *zarzuelas*. Diaghilev said of Ravel's *La Valse* that it was not so much a ballet as the portrait of a ballet: in the same way, *España* is a portrait of Spanish music by a brilliant apprentice. Albeniz hated the work, and Falla liked it little better, although he was more Francophile in his sympathies. It is of course true that the trappings of *España* come from a large Parisian store. To my mind, it is that which gives this ingenious Spanish fantasy its essential charm. Chabrier moreover declared in the programme that it was a mingling and superimposing of the musical essence of North and South, and

[1] Tragically famous at this time because of a mining disaster.

Life and Work

as laconically as Ravel he would add: "It's a piece in F, that's all".

After leaving the Ministry, Chabrier became from 1881 a sort of chorus-master and manager of the new concerts conducted by Charles Lamoureux. Chabrier dedicated *España* to this conductor whose whole life was spent making known his music.

On Sunday, 4 November, 1883, Lamoureux conducted *España* for the first time. So immediate and rapturous was its success that the work had to be repeated the following Sunday, 11 November, as well as on 20 and 27 February, 1884.

Chabrier became famous overnight, and his rhapsody enjoyed the same popularity as Ravel's *Bolero* today. Baker-boys and milliners' assistants hummed *España* on the streets or on the platforms of buses. Even the stiffest musicians could not resist the flood of sunshine which suddenly pierced the frequent sullen greyness of the Sunday concerts. Its orchestration, moreover, created a completely new climate. A long time was to elapse before Stravinsky recalled the famous trombones of *España*:

Chevillard at once made a transcription for 8 hands, Messager for 4 hands, while Waldteufel made from it a suite of waltzes for use in the *brasseries*.

1883 and 1884 were particularly fruitful years for Chabrier. He was certainly helped by a fortunate circumstance. His model mother-in-law, Mme Dejean, realizing that her son-in-law needed peaceful working conditions, and perhaps also aware of the progress of his hidden illness, so resistant to cure, decided in 1883 to rent a house at La Membrolle, near Tours.

Emmanuel Chabrier

From then onwards, Chabrier spent long months there, from Easter to October. The greater part of the output of this Parisian from Auvergne was in fact composed in Touraine!

The house is on the main road from Tours to Le Mans, and is extremely commonplace. It is a brick house suitable for a retired butcher, of the kind to be seen, storm-threatened and snow-covered, in so many of Vlaminck's paintings. Like many collectors of paintings, Chabrier had no idea of setting, and adored this vast house for its comfort and its large garden, where he could rest during his work. He also often went on shopping expeditions to Tours.

Right from the very first letter written from La Membrolle, it is clear he was in his element. This is how he writes to his wife, who in June 1883 had stayed in Paris to make several small purchases and final holiday arrangements:

> It is charming here. I arrived yesterday at 4.30. Your mother met us with her *quart de bonne*. Mutual pleasure at seeing each other again. This morning I've already installed a linen table with X-shaped trestles in the front room. The table I've dreamt of, two metres long and one metre thirty wide. That should be big enough for orchestration. There ought to be room for the orchestra itself. . . . My bedroom looks out on the garden, and my study on the main road.
>
> In ten minutes' time the gardener is going to give me a shower. I'll stand in the bath-tub near the stove, and the operation ought to be a great success.

Once again, of course, the faithful Nanine had followed her Mavel. In this peaceful atmosphere, in the summer of 1883, Chabrier composed his *Trois valses romantiques*. He wrote them gleefully, as may be seen from this postcard in the form of a riddle, sent to his publisher Costallat:

– bird which decks itself in peacock feathers (geai=jay)
– nature of a being called Carabosse (fée=fairy)

Life and Work

– note of the scale (la).
– place where there was a wooden horse (Troie=Troy)
– mediocre painter of Piazza San Marco, Venice (Ziem)
– mineral water (Vals)
Ha-Ha!
[=J'ai fait la troisième valse!]

The *Valses romantiques* are some of the most perfect things Chabrier has written. His melodic invention is only equalled by his extraordinary pianistic sense and feeling for harmony. This orchestral piano-writing is all the more refreshing because of the academic nature of piano-writing at the time, be it by Saint-Saëns or by d'Indy. Chabrier, what is more, was fully aware of his success. On 4 September, 1883, he wrote to Paul Lacôme: "I think they might even sell. There is not much music for two pianos; young girls who take the piano seriously (need I add they're generally the ugly ones) will be able to ask for them".

Technically difficult, the interpretation of these waltzes is very exacting. Claude Rostand has rightly said that they need careful preparation but have to be played "as if they were being improvised, with a cigar in the mouth and a glass of brandy on the piano". I would like to suggest appropriate metronomic markings not included in the printed edition, as I often had the pleasure of playing them with Messager, who gave them their first performance with the composer at the Société Nationale on 15 December 1883.

The first waltz ($\dotted{\quarter}$=88) has to be played quite straight, the second ($\quarter$=112-120) very *rubato*. As for the third, I know that it is very difficult to establish the right tempo. A tempo which neither drags nor runs away with itself ($\dotted{\quarter}$=84) would seem to be the right one. The tone-colour needs careful attention, and plenty of pedal should be used. Ideally the effect should be one of sensuousness, akin to that of Renoir's *Fillettes au piano*.

Emmanuel Chabrier

From 1879, Chabrier was working on *Gwendoline*. The autograph libretto bears the date of 10 March, 1879. Evidently the text was frequently revised, but from then onwards, the composer had it constantly in mind.

I will leave discussion of this work until the next chapter, and end by saying something about *La Sulamite*, a cantata for mezzo-soprano, female chorus and orchestra. Completed in 1884, the work was first performed on 15 March, 1885 in the Salle du Château d'Eau at the Concerts Lamoureux, Mme Brunet-Lafleur being the soloist. The poem, by Jean Richepin, is obviously no masterpiece, but as Chabrier was never fortunate in his collaborators, there is no particular cause for complaint on this occasion. *La Sulamite* is one of his most richly-scored orchestral pieces. Perhaps the orchestration is a little heavy for the voice, but is the subject so important that every word needs to be understood?

Alfred Bruneau gives a summary of it in an inflated style which is well-suited to Richepin's poem:

> It is a long cry of love, formidable in its last paroxysm. The memory of the beloved, at first so vague and soft, like a soft breeze, escapes from happy lips, which begin singing of the conquering power of eyes, teeth, mane [sic!] and golden skin, under devouring and caressing suns. It is a triumphant Hosanna which in its gradual intoxication of sound opens for us the Paradise gates to feminine religions, deadly and eternal...

Why is *La Sulamite* so rarely sung? It clearly needs a big personality to do it justice. In our day, Rita Gorr would carry it off with ease.

III

GWENDOLINE – LE ROI MALGRÉ LUI – SOUVENIR DE MUNICH – HABANERA

To write an opera! To be performed at the Opéra! Such had been Chabrier's dream since the age of twenty, but at this period, alas, the gates of the Opéra were zealously guarded by officials and academics.

One is dumbfounded to discover what was being performed at the Opéra at this time, apart from Saint-Saëns, Massenet, Gounod and Delibes! I imagine that political support alone made possible the inclusion of so many names, today forgotten. When one realises that Godard was preferred before Chabrier! The latter naturally frequented the brilliant salons of Mesdames de Gabriac, Greffulhe, de Narbonne Lara, de Polignac, but that was no certain way of forcing the doors of the State Theatres.

Although Chabrier had no illusions about all this, he set eagerly to work. He wrote to Edouard Moullé, who had criticized the rather ponderous form of *Gwendoline*:

> I entirely agree with you: *Gwendoline* is a sort of musical *Liebig*;[1] it is too concentrated. I should have mixed some pellets of it into a straightforward liquid, and stirred before serving, but I write without ambition, without an immediate goal: I don't think I shall ever see it performed.

All the same, after much gruelling labour, Chabrier put the final touches on 12 June, 1885.

Gwendoline was refused in Paris, but given its première at

[1] Justus Liebig (1803-1873), chemist and nutritional expert: a famous maker of meat essence (Trans.).

Emmanuel Chabrier

La Monnaie in Brussels on 10 April, 1886. Fragments however had been well received at the Concerts Lamoureux on 9 and 22 November, 1885.

At Brussels, the opera had an immediate success, but as usual Chabrier was pursued by ill-luck, and had the mournful experience of seeing his work withdrawn after two performances. The Director, Monsieur Verdhurt, had drawn up his schedule without government subsidy. Thanks to his Wagnerian tenor friend, Van Dyck, who had introduced Chabrier to the conductor Felix Mottl, Musical Director at the Grand-Ducal Theatre in Karlsruhe, *Gwendoline* enjoyed some success in Germany. Between 1889 and 1891 it was staged at Karlsruhe, Leipzig, Dresden, Munich, Stuttgart and Düsseldorf, but had to wait until April 1893 to be performed in France ... and then at Lyons.

In 1888 a moving private hearing took place in the salon of the Princesse de Polignac, then Princesse de Scey-Montbéliard. On 7 April, 1888, Chabrier wrote to Van Dyck:

> A complete hearing for *Gwendoline* is to be given on 8th and 15th May at the house of a very rich lady, with Madame Lureau-Escalaïs, Melchissedec, twenty-four choristers, double quartet, harp, harmonium (Fauré), piano (me) conductor (Gabriel Marie), percussion (d'Indy and Messager). It looks like being a very elegant affair, and, *huge secret, keep it dark, only you know,* as I am negotiating very seriously with the Opéra, I have taken the advice of this lady (Princesse de Scey-Montbéliard, née Singer), and have chosen people from the Opéra who can play the roles as and when opportunity offers.

Unfortunately, in spite of such enthusiastic support, this run-through did not bring about the anticipated result, and, Chabrier had to wait until 20 December, 1893 for the Opéra—then under the directorship of Gaillard and Bertrand—to stage *Gwendoline.*

Life and Work

It was a triumphant success. The audience gave Chabrier a tremendous ovation, and he had several times to acknowledge the applause from the front of his box.

By then he was no longer jovial-looking, but a wan-looking man with a ravaged face, who smiled almost without knowing why.

Sometimes he would forget that the opera was his, and leaning towards his neighbour would murmur: "It's good, it's really very good," as if he were talking about someone else's opera. This is reminiscent of Ravel, who came out of the Salle Pleyel in 1936 after a triumphant performance of *Daphnis et Chloé* murmuring, whether he realized it or not: "But this chap Ravel really had talent".

I have spoken so ill of the libretto of *Gwendoline* that I must summarize it here:

The action takes place in some part of Great Britain during the eighth century. The Danes have just conquered the Saxons. Gwendoline is the daughter of the Saxon chief. She is given in marriage to Harald, the Danish chief, who has been immediately struck by her beauty. But Gwendoline's father Armel orders her to kill Harald in his sleep on the bridal night.

Gwendoline falls in love with Harald, and prepares to escape with him, when he is killed by the Saxons, who have been forewarned by Armel. Both "die standing, proudly, without falling [sic] in their bloody apotheosis" (the stage direction is Mendès' own).

If the plot were all, it might still pass, but what about the text, particularly at the end, where Gwendoline and Harald succumb—naturally in terms of Wagnerian ritual?

> Gwendoline and Harald: O God, receive us, the hour is nigh for us to wing our way on a white steed to wondrous Valhalla.

Emmanuel Chabrier

Gwendoline: In the ocean I shall become a Valkyrie in a golden helmet.

Harald: Thou in the ocean shalt become . . .

Despite all this balderdash, *Gwendoline* remains a masterpiece, which brilliant casting and a modern production might easily bring back to life.

There are many things to quote from this astonishing score. First, the Overture, with its fevered lyricism, and its exuberant 'cellos. Then in the first act, Gwendoline's narration, Harald's colourful aria, and the spinning chorus, not so strongly influenced by the *Flying Dutchman* as was made out. The spinning wheel is entirely responsible.

Another exquisite section is when Harald asks Armel for his daughter's hand: "Old man"—what a discourteous way of addressing your future father-in-law—"old man, give me your daughter".

The prelude to the second act is full of tenderness, then comes the gem of the score, the *epithalamium*. Chabrier forgets all about Northern mists, the eighth century, and the hemp matting, to draw from his inner depths a music so pure and luminous that I am tempted to call it Attic.

A surprise awaits us on page 202 (3rd system) of the piano score. If Arkel is substituted for Armel, the first two bars might well come from *Pelléas*. Here is proof positive of Debussy's admiration for Chabrier:

Life and Work

The following duet is very beautiful, suddenly broken into by a male chorus in the wings. This is astonishingly stark, outlined as it is in major and minor sixths:

[musical notation: Tenor and Bass parts marked "Ah!"]

The last scene is less inventive, but still shows magnificent orchestral tension.

I am the fortunate owner of Vincent d'Indy's score, containing a dedication by Chabrier: "To my dear good friend Vincent d'Indy, his sincere admirer (no trace of G. or M.)". These initials are poor concealment for Gounod and Massenet. They serve to emphasize the gap which separated the members of the "Institut des Indépendants".

After the première of *Gwendoline* at Brussels, Chabrier began casting around for a new libretto. His far-sighted friends Lacôme and Messager hoped he would make a return to a frivolous subject, as in the days of *L'Étoile*, but Chabrier had the Opéra-Comique in mind, where a work as light as *L'Étoile* would never at that time have been staged. Once again, he chose a bad libretto. In 1882, Najac and Burani had made a three-act libretto called *Le Roi malgré lui* from a very mediocre piece by Ancelot. Discussions between librettists and musicians were protracted. To judge from the evidence and the autograph libretto, Jean Richepin collaborated closely in its production. Chabrier assumed things were settled, and set to work in spring 1886. After much intensive effort, he completed it in the early months of 1887. The première took place on 18 May, 1887 at the Opéra-Comique.

At last Chabrier had been allowed across the threshold.

Emmanuel Chabrier

I have been allowed to consult the huge file comprising the libretto of *Le Roi malgré lui* in the Bretton-Chabrier archives, and so have been able to form a pretty accurate idea of the difficulties involved in its realization.

For irrefutable proof that Chabrier nourished few illusions about his collaborators, it is sufficient to reproduce the note on the cover containing the mass of scattered papers written by Najac, Burani, Richepin, and Chabrier himself:

> Manuscript by three authors (and even me). The genesis of *Le Roi malgré lui*. There's a little of everything here: a bouillabaisse by Najac and Burani, cooked by Richepin, with the seasoning thrown in by me. An astonishing document. More like a battle-ground.

It opens with an outline of the work and even part of the text, beautifully hand-written by M. Leduc (literary and dramatic copyist—48 rue Laffite, Paris), which Najac and Burani had sent off to the composer. On the grey-blue cover to Act I, Chabrier has written: "Libretto, assuming this work *has to be made* into an operetta! my remarks are illuminating!..." After that comes a mass of loose papers ceaselessly exchanged between Chabrier and his librettists.

It was fortunate that Chabrier had a feeling for movement, as everything Najac sent him was incredibly static. Act I, for instance, opens with a long, nonsensical duet between two Polish conspirators. Chabrier asked for it to move. "Get a move on, get a move on," he wrote in the margin of a sheet sent him by Burani.

Chabrier finally got what he wanted, to wit "a very lively opening scene"—the game of dice for the French noblemen (*Cinq, trois, j'ai gagné, j'ai perdu*). Immediately afterwards Chabrier insisted on an *air gai* (for Fritelli, who was originally called Alamani).

Chabrier disliked the first version so much that he wrote in the margin: "There's a bit of everything here. I stuck my finger in it too. Poof! What a dreadful mess! Mere patchwork."

At this point the supremely arrogant writing of Jean Richepin puts in an appearance, written not on scraps of quarto as before, but on superb white vellum. It was in fact Richepin who produced the definitive version of Fritelli's Polish verses, showing that Chabrier had had to appeal to him from the beginning.

As the score begins to take shape, it is clear that Richepin is doing more than merely correct Najac and Burani. The following are all in Richepin's hand, often with Chabrier's corrections: the verses for Minka, the air for the King (*Cher pays du gai soleil*), and the duet for Minka and the King (*Je l'aime de toute mon âme*) in the first act: the Barcarolle in the second act, and the duet for Alexina and Minka in the third.

As an example of what happened, Chabrier sent back to Richepin the manuscript of the Barcarolle Duet with the following comment:

> There is an error in this duet after Alexina's furious outburst, *Oui, je vous hais*. I haven't got enough time to make something of Henri's entry: *Souvenez-vous* comes *too soon*. Give me five or six lines more, in addition to what's already there, making ten lines altogether before *souvenez-vous*.

It seems likely that Richepin gave up this patching of someone else's libretto, since in the third act Chabrier's writing takes over. Chabrier remarks in the margin of a scene: "He'd had enough of it. But he went on making sudden swoops".

Unfortunately all this joint labour served only to produce a feeble libretto, which has always militated against the success of the work as a whole. As is clear from the following:

In the first act, the curtain rises on the state-room of the Royal Palace. Henri III has just arrived in Poland, where he is about to be crowned. With the exception of Nangis, who is susceptible to the charms of Polish women, his companions are all nostalgic for France. Fritelli, a sort of Italian ambassador, is not at all happy about the situation (this comic role was played in masterly fashion by Lucien Fugère).

Entry of Minka, badgered by some over-zealous soldiery. Nangis gallantly stands up for her, and falls in love. Minka then sings a very charming song. Henri confesses that he is missing France. Minka tells him that she loves the French, and, unaware that she is talking to the King, tells him that there are rumblings of revolt. Fritelli is horrified, despite the blandishments of his adventuress companion, the lovely Alexina. For his part, Henri is delighted, because he longs to return to Paris. He will help the conspirators get rid of him. Alexina is also unaware of Henri's identity, but she remembers having met him in Venice, and promises to help him.

In the second act, Henri, disguised as Nangis, arrives at the Laski Palace for a ball. To the sound of a Barcarolle, he evokes his Venetian affair with Alexina. A passionate duet between Nangis and Minka is interrupted by the arrival of the conspirators, who take Nangis for the King. Henri orders him to keep up the pretence. But events turn out badly, because Laski wants to kill his prisoner. Happily the French guard arrives in time, and Henri swears to Laski to see that the King is expelled just the same.

This duly happens in the third act, in an inn near Cracow, where the court is awaited, prior to its return to France. Fritelli has come on ahead, Minka is desperate because she assumes Nangis to be the King, and is afraid that he has been assassinated. Amidst general rejoicing Nangis arrives, and tells the whole story. The two lovers are free to enjoy their love. Despite himself, Henri has suddenly been voted King of Poland by general plebiscite.

Ravel often used to say to me: "The première of *Le Roi malgré lui* changed the direction of harmony in France". That is literally true, because chords like these, heard for the first

Life and Work

time, served as a guide to Debussy and Ravel. I would also add that although I consider Satie to be the second precursor of the French School, it is worth realizing that his *Sarabandes*, dating from autumn 1887, show the influence of *Le Roi*, first performed on 18 May. As is apparent in these examples:

[Musical notation: CHABRIER - Le Roi malgré lui, ppp]

[Musical notation: SATIE - 2ᵉ Sarabande, p]

Debussy and Ravel were also influenced by the orchestration of *Le Roi malgré lui*. It is necessary to remember the instrumental climate of the period. Saint-Saëns was justly considered a model of perfect orchestration: perfect, certainly, but entirely conventional. Chabrier, on the other hand, took entirely opposing sounds and mixed them together with rare delight.

Some passages, notably Fritelli's broad comedy, bring this *opéra-comique* closer to *opéra-bouffe*. Let us not complain.

The role of Minka, created by Odette Isaac, is delightfully fresh: Alexina's is less striking, but includes the extraordinarily charming Barcarolle Duet with the King. There are many other ravishing numbers, such as the Gipsy song, and the Nocturne for two voices in the third act, but the obvious centrepiece of the work is the masterly *Fête polonaise*.

Even in its concert version (without chorus), the *Fête polonaise* is intoxicating in its rhythm, its instrumental verve and its constant waves of tenderness which break out all the way through the piece.

Although it did not give rise to the same enthusiasm as was later to greet *Gwendoline*, *Le Roi* was very well received at the Opéra-Comique, until a fire on 25 May put a sudden stop to its career there after only three performances, on May 18, 21 and 23, 1887.

It was revived on 18 November, 1887, at the Théâtre des Nations, where the Opéra-Comique had taken refuge. But after eleven performances, it disappeared entirely from the hoardings. Chabrier consoled himself for these blows of fate with countless performances of *Le Roi* in Germany. Thanks to the faithful Mottl, there were productions in Karlsruhe, Dresden, Munich, and Cologne, giving Chabrier a pretext to make frequent trips across the Rhine.

But let it not be assumed that Chabrier's music is popular in Germany. On the contrary, there are few countries where it is more completely unknown. In mounting *Gwendoline* and *Le Roi*, German theatre directors were in effect thanking Chabrier for his devotion to Wagner. As it happened, Chabrier had helped Lamoureux to stage the famous performance of *Lohengrin* at the Théâtre Eden on 3 May, 1887, in the middle of rehearsals for *Le Roi*. The performance had no follow-up, because of frenzied public outcry, and a violent press campaign.

Mottl gave Chabrier the only chance of surviving in Germany by orchestrating, perhaps over-heavily, the *Bourrée fantasque* and the *Trois valses romantiques*: these are sometimes played on German radios.

I would now like to mention an extraordinary little work written at the same time: *Souvenir de Munich*, quadrille for piano (four hands) on familiar themes from *Tristan und Isolde*. This minor work sheds profound light on Chabrier's humorous and creative gifts. He was far gone in Wagner worship, but when it came to having a good laugh, he was the first to enjoy himself. So spontaneous, so good-humoured was Chabrier that one could not possibly call the piece sacrilegious. For him, whole-hearted admiration did not exclude plain-speaking.

Henri Pourrat tells a very good story: on 19 July, 1889, Chabrier was invited to a reception by Madame Wagner after returning from gathering a laurel branch from Wagner's tomb (a branch he kept all his life). Tea was served, along with some heavy pastries. Chabrier dug his teeth into one, made a face and said to Pourrat: "Quelle cochonnerie (=How disgusting)! Loathsome! Whatever can I do with it?" Retreating backwards to one of the master's chests, Chabrier opened a drawer and slipped the cake inside, regardless of any clothes which might still be lying there.

Souvenir de Munich is irresistibly funny. Tristan's principal themes appear with false noses and added beards, all except the theme of the love duet which is scarcely altered (all the same!!). The strange thing is that what emerges is 100% Chabrier, just as Velasquez' court darlings, seen by Picasso, emerge as pure Picasso.

Personally, I find this quadrille enchanting. A *Habanera* for piano, later orchestrated, dates from the same period. It is a fascinating piece, which shows that Chabrier's counterpoint is generally conceived as "counter-melody".[1]

And so a happy period came to an end. The years that followed, alas, were to close in very quickly.

[1] French: *contrechant* (Trans.).

IV

JOYEUSE MARCHE – SONGS – BRISEÏS – BOURRÉE FANTASQUE – LAST YEARS – DEATH

In 1888, Chabrier found himself famous. On 13 July, he was awarded the Légion d'honneur, which one may be sure pleased him greatly. He conducted occasionally in the provinces, at Bordeaux and Angers. The Artistic Association of Angers, founded in 1875, was at this time far and away the boldest in the composition of its programmes. In 1884, less than a year after the Paris performance, Chabrier had conducted *España* there. On 4 November, 1888, he returned with unpublished works: *Marche française*, *Habanera* and the *Suite pastorale*.

Although the *Habanera* and the *Suite pastorale* (*Idylle*, *Danse villageoise*, *Sous-bois* and *Scherzo valse*) were no more than orchestrated piano pieces, the *Marche française*, although taken from an unpublished rondo for four hands, was an original piece for orchestra, and what a fascinating piece at that!

As the title of *Marche française* had already been deposited at the Société des Auteurs, it was called *Joyeuse marche* when Lamoureux first performed it in Paris on 16 February, 1890. A charming design by Chéret graced the cover of the published edition. A joyous mid-Lenten crowd are coming down the hill of Montmartre, holding Basque tambourines in their hands, exactly as the music suggests. Never before, I think, had Chabrier ventured so far in orchestral invention. It would be interesting to know what Saint-Saëns thought of it. Not all

Life and Work

that badly perhaps, if we remember the *Carnaval des Animaux*. After all, that suspicious composer only feared what he construed as competition, and here there was no question of a symphony.

In the summer of 1889, Chabrier went to Bayreuth to hear *Parsifal*, *Tristan* and *Die Meistersinger*. On 22 July, he wrote to his wife: "Today, at four o'clock, rehearsal of *Meistersinger*. It's marvellous. I wept like a child!" By the end of twenty-four hours, he was a familiar figure, if for no better reason than for the unlikely cotton nightcap he always wore. He used to say of it: "It's as comfortable at night as it is for travelling, walking in the street, or going to the theatre."

And what did he compose on his return from Bayreuth? Six exquisite songs, which cocked as many irreverent snooks at his idol's aesthetic outlook. It is good that Chabrier was able to achieve such a flight of fantasy, given that at this time Vincent d'Indy was bogged down in *Fervaal*.

These six songs, composed in 1890, are miraculous illustrations of Chabrier's purest style. To tell the truth, he never felt at ease except in songs based on rhyming stanzas. Meticulous prosody was not for him. Thus the light verses of Rosemonde Gérard or Edmond Rostand stimulated him as much as if they had been intended for an operetta.

I have always been sorry that he never collaborated with Rostand. What a masterpiece a *Cyrano de Bergerac* by Chabrier might have been! However comically he handles the *Villanelle* of the little ducks, the *Ballade* of the big turkeys, the *Pastorale* of the pink pigs, or the grasshoppers, there is always a deep country sense discernible in Chabrier's music. The same sensibility, the same poetic perception shows itself whether it is the melting sound of the Angelus, or the march of the big turkey lawyers (its *ritornello* irresistibly reminiscent of Don Giovanni's Serenade).

Paradoxically, what makes the interpretation of these songs perilous is that their irony must never mask the poetry,

Emmanuel Chabrier

deceptively facile. Chabrier wrote to Van Dyck of *Toutes les fleurs*: "I am also going to send you some songs, one of which is dedicated to my Nénest. It's an irresistible *baveux de salon*." By *"baveux de salon"* he certainly did not intend the merciless pejorative sense (salon drivel (diarrhoea!)) which has since been attributed to it. We may be sure that Chabrier "believed" in his songs, just as all true musicians believe in them today.

Dedicated for the most part to *demi-caractère* singers such as Jeanne Granier, Mily Meyer and Lucien Fugère, it is quite clear what kind of interpretation Chabrier hoped his songs would receive.

Hostile to the "côté Verdurin" of certain salons on the Plaine Monceau, Chabrier did nothing to court the approval of the wealthy bourgeois ladies who sang the early songs of Fauré, sometimes extremely well—I am thinking here of Mme Bardac-Debussy. His world was the theatre, and he meant to stay there.

Perfect interpreters of these little masterpieces, half-way between the stage and the concert platform, have been rare indeed. Foremost amongst them was Reynaldo Hahn, who sang *L'Île heureuse* enchantingly, accompanying himself at the piano, and giving it the controlled relaxation which it needs: this *Embarquement pour Cythère*, a setting of a rather ordinary poem by Ephraïm Mikhaël, typical of the 1890's, contains the essence of Chabrier's song-writing.

Another great interpreter was Jane Bathori, wife of Emile Engel—creator of the role of Armel at La Monnaie in Brussels—who gave the best of her art to difficult causes. Many songs by Debussy and Ravel owe their first performance to an artist who consistently fought for the proper recognition of Chabrier. In recent times, Roger Bourdin and Pierre Bernac have done the same.

Two further perfect achievements need to be mentioned: *Chanson pour Jeanne* (1886) and Chabrier's last song, *Lied*,

Life and Work

this time an almost wicked setting of light verse by Mendès. There is rare imaginative quality in this charming fantasy featuring undergrowth, strawberries, an elf with a delicate moustache, and a very sharp-witted girl. I know nothing more impertinent in the whole of French song.

1890 was a good year for Chabrier for it saw the composition of the *Ode à la musique*, written for the "inauguration" of his friend Jules Griset's apartment, an astonishing masterpiece setting a poem by Rostand, who was also a friend of Griset. The first hearing took place privately, at the end of November, 1890, with Chabrier at the piano. In its later version, it was performed on 22 January, 1893, at a concert of the Conservatoire. In this perfect work, one is at a loss to know which to praise most: the melodic invention, the harmonic texture, or the tender orchestration.

The following anecdote was related to me by Ingelbrecht, that loyal supporter of Chabrier. At the inaugural concert of the Théâtre des Champs-Elysées on 2 April, 1913, Ingelbrecht began his programme with the *Ode à la musique*. Debussy had come to hear the last rehearsal. He made some comments to the young conductor at the end of the *Ode*, and Ingelbrecht began it again. Later he came up to Debussy to know if he was satisfied, and the latter said smilingly: "It was all right the first time, but I love the music so much I wanted to hear it twice."

From 1890 onwards, everything closed in round Chabrier. Some months earlier, his faithful housekeeper Nanine had become paralysed, and had had to be taken to a sanatorium at Arcueil, where she died on 15 January, 1891. He was struck to the heart by the loss of a woman who had brought him up from childhood.

Another event which affected him deeply was the death of Franck, who died at the age of 68 on 8 November, 1890, after an attack of pleurisy. Chabrier had never belonged to Franck's group of pupils, but for him Franck represented benevolent respectability. He was chosen by the members of the Société Nationale to speak in their name at the funeral. Administrators of the Ministry of Fine Arts and the Conservatoire did not even deign to be represented.

Probably Saint-Saëns was responsible for much of this indescribable attitude; at the age of eighteen, in 1917, I had the cheek (there is no other word) to ask Debussy, Roussel, d'Indy, Dukas, Ropartz, Satie and Blanche Selva what they thought of César Franck. From Saint-Saëns I received the following reply:

Dear Sir,

Perhaps the same will happen to César Franck as happened to Richard Wagner, about whose music people have been asking my opinion for the last forty years. Franck had great talent, and I myself gave him a chance to display it by persuading Jules Simon, the then Minister of Fine Arts, to give him the organ classes at the Conservatoire, which had been offered to me. This meant that Franck no longer had to waste his time giving piano lessons to earn his living, and was able to concentrate on composition.

It was made out that this great talent amounted to genius: I entertained no such notion. But in spite of my ideas, in spite of questionnaires, César Franck by now belongs to posterity. In the last resort, it will be posterity which judges whether he deserves a crown of gold or of silver.

With my sincere good wishes,
C. SAINT-SAËNS.

From summer 1866 onwards, Chabrier talks in his letters of nothing but *Briseïs*, an opera in three acts on a libretto by Ephraïm Mikhaël and Mendès which "runs away with him" [*sic*]. Once again, one is dumbfounded by the choice.

A summary of the first act runs as follows: in Corinth, at the time of the Emperor Hadrian, the blonde Briseïs is betrothed to the fisherman Hilas. Her mother, Thanasto, suffers from a mysterious disease. Thanasto, who is a Christian, prays God to heal her so that she can convert her daughter.

A catechist opportunely presents himself. He exhorts Briseïs to become Christian to save her mother. Briseïs consents. General rejoicing. Curtain.

I do not know what would have happened in the following acts, but I doubt whether a libretto of this kind could have found favour with the public. Nothing daunted, Chabrier set to work with his customary enthusiasm, and the single act of his opera completed in 1891 contains extraordinarily beautiful things. More than ever before, these long supple melodies in 9/8 and 12/8 float with natural perfection over harmonies which are more and more refined. Some pages could easily have been composed in 1910, particularly from the point of view of the orchestral writing. In the shape in which it has been left to us, *Briseïs* can be best appreciated in concert performance. Fortunately in our own day Inglebrecht has been its faithful champion. It is to be hoped that a conductor of the younger generation may follow in his footsteps.

It was in fact in concert form that Lamoureux originally performed *Briseïs* in January, 1897, arousing enthusiasm amongst all the connoisseurs, whether their names were Charpentier and Bruneau, or Debussy and Ravel.

From 1891 onwards, Chabrier's health gradually declined. In spite of this he found strength to write some piano pieces, which were published after his death, and above all that masterpiece known as the *Bourrée Fantasque*.

Written just before he went under, the *Bourrée Fantasque* is as young and impetuous as *España*. It is dedicated to the pianist Edouard Risler, and from a pianistic point of view is as full of innovations as Debussy's *Études*, or Ravel's *Gaspard de la nuit*. Like Liszt's *Mephisto Valse*, it shows us Chabrier's prodigious knowledge of the piano. A letter to d'Indy, thanking him for having sent him the *Poème des montagnes*, shows the extent to which Chabrier understood his craft, in spite of the element of improvisation so often present in his music:

1881

Thank you, my friend, for sending me your *Poème des montagnes*, which I find exquisite. Above all, the part about the "heath", all the mist which would sound splendid with orchestra, and all the fresh air. I also love the "A deux", and the whole of the ending. I'm less fond of the "danses rythmiques": they're singular in their writing first of all, and undoubtedly in their rhythm, but these rhythms are too cut-up by *passages for left thumb*, by effects which *crowd one on top of the other*, and *show such little design in their disorder*, that I have no time to be either surprised or ravished: the piece is over before I have been able to enter into it. Do I make myself clear, or is it perhaps I who am an innocent idiot?

With its mixture of brutality and tenderness, the whole of Chabrier is to be found in the *Bourrée Fantasque*. As comic effects have no part in such music, there is no reason to drag out the Bourrée's central episode. It is another piece which should be played more or less straight. Robert Casadesus is today one of its most remarkable interpreters.

Chabrier began orchestrating the *Bourrée Fantasque* shortly after finishing it. Roland-Manuel (a fervent Chabrier enthusiast, who has acquired the composer's desk) owns the autograph, which is remarkable in every way. In the first place, the orchestration is very reduced: a piccolo, flute, oboe, two B flat clarinets, bassoon, two horns, two cornets in C, a trombone, percussion (kettle-drum, side-drum, triangle, bass drum, cymbals) and piano. Mottl's orchestration, on the contrary, is massively ostentatious. Whereas Chabrier orchestrates the opening theme in a strict unison of two clarinets, bassoon, viola and 'cellos, Mottl mobilizes horns, harp, pizzicato violins, etc.:

Life and Work

The extraordinary instrumental intuition of the composer of *España* can never be sufficiently praised.

The second theme is set out in a very unexpected way, with a low-lying flute and a high-lying bassoon, in unison:

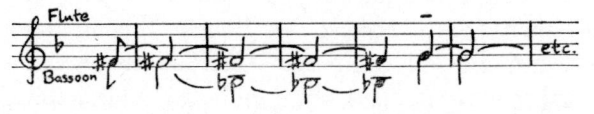

The fact that Chabrier always composed at the piano—as did Debussy and Stravinsky—did not prevent him from finding a rare orchestral colour: a unique achievement at a time when Franck, d'Indy and Saint-Saëns hardly ever emerged from well-worn paths.

In the long letter to René Martineau from which I have already quoted, Henri Duparc on 15 January, 1908 made some valuable comments on this subject. Although I do not entirely agree with him in that I consider Chabrier was already a master of orchestration at the time of *L'Étoile* and *L'Éducation manquée*, I would like to quote these lines to show how perfectly he understood the problem:

> What is perhaps most interesting from a biographical point of view is that Chabrier had a kind of sudden revelation of orchestral colour. What caused it? Was it something he had read? something he had heard? I don't know. All the same, he seemed at the beginning to lack an orchestral sense, a gift which cannot be acquired. Some time before *España* (I don't remember the exact year, but as I remember he was still living in rue Mosnier), he orchestrated some of the delightful piano pieces he had just written, and showed the orchestration to some friends, of

Emmanuel Chabrier

whom I was one. It was frankly mediocre, a pianist's orchestration (I believe done at the piano). It was heavy, clumsy, and monotonous to such an extent that I came away distressed, for I loved Chabrier dearly. I told myself that the dear boy would probably never bring to his orchestration that extraordinary personality which is like a signature in all his music. Like so many other people he clearly knew how to orchestrate, but nothing more. Upon which we left for our various destinations, I to the country and he for Spain. He returned with this dazzling *España*, this masterpiece of orchestration, and from that time his orchestration has never been inferior. It might even be said to have improved, in the sense that it came to fit the music more perfectly: *España* gives me the impression of a marvellously *orchestrated* piece: the works which follow seem to have been *conceived for orchestra*. I am not even aware of the orchestration, which is at one with the idea, and cannot be imagined any other way.

Nothing in fact is less interchangeable than Chabrier's orchestral colour. At the same time it surprises and delights us. As time went on, its echo could be heard in *Petrouchka*, and in the works of certain composers of my own generation.

To me it seems beyond doubt that Chabrier's taste for bold tonal relationships resulted from his love for the Impressionist painters, because the music demonstrates an undeniable affinity with some of the pictures.

The five posthumous pieces (*Aubade, Ballabile, Caprice, Feuillet d'album*, and *Ronde champêtre*), Chabrier's last works for piano, all achieve their purpose, but *Ballabile* and the *Feuillet d'album* are of very rare quality. *Ballabile* recalls with its freshness the *Lied* for voice and piano, whilst *Feuillet d'album*, with its doubling of the melody at the octave, a device of which he was so fond, is perhaps Chabrier's most tender music.

Life and Work

Lastly, I should also mention an *Air de ballet* for piano (an old work), which is as acute as a rough sketch of a dancer by Degas. For lazy ears, this piece might seem to be vintage Chaminade. From the outset, the play on major and minor reveals a subtle ear.

From 1891 onwards, Chabrier slowly declined. Little by little, the general paralysis affected all the nervous centres. This secret and very long-standing disease takes a sudden turn for the worse when the sufferer is around fifty. Chabrier became incapable of working, and questions of hydrotherapy, régime and cures suddenly began to claim the whole of his attention. Little by little he vanished from the places where he had been the life and soul of the party. "I am sick, and like the animals I am hiding away," he wrote to a friend.

According to Messager, he was able to play the piano for quite some time after this, but could not concentrate on any creative work. It may be remembered how it was an automaton who acknowledged the applause at the first performance of *Gwendoline*. From then on, he declined day by day, his marvellous intelligence foundering in a total vagueness. On 12 September, 1894, at the age of fifty-three, he died in his apartment at 13 avenue Trudaine, in the presence of his wife and his two sons.

The funeral service was held at Notre-Dame-de-Lorette. This great musician had hoped to be buried in the cemetery at Passy, close to his friend Manet, but it proved impossible to purchase a plot.

So it is that the composer who brought tenderness and joy into French music lies buried in the cemetery of Montparnasse (No. 25 West, 4th line South, 90th division).

Dear Chabrier, how we all love you!

September/November 1959, Noizay.

In Memoriam
Tributes from Contemporary Musicians

IN MEMORIAM
Tributes from Contemporary Musicians

In 1897, at the request of Mendès, the publishing house of Enoch printed forty special copies of *Briseïs* on imperial Japanese paper,[1] over and above the regular edition. This formed a posthumous *hommage à Chabrier*: it contained a very feeble sketch by Puvis de Chavannes, an excellent portrait—an etching—by Desmoulins, the entire text of *Briseïs*, letters from musicians of very varied leanings, and finally, poems.

Of these tributes I have chosen the most obviously significant, and of the poems, those by Charles Van Lerberghe, Henri de Régnier, Francis Viélé-Griffin, and in particular the magnificent sonnet by Saint-Pol-Roux.

We know how deeply Chabrier was touched by the esteem in which his colleagues held him: I believe he would have been even more touched by the garlands which the poets laid on his tomb—particularly so, as in a very curious letter of 1891 to Verlaine's publisher (a letter I possess, thanks to the generosity of my friend Willemetz) he wrote: "If the book by Verlaine—an old friend of twenty-eight years' standing—comes out this month, please ask him to put his great paw on the first page for me."

As he so often said himself, Chabrier was certainly "the least illiterate" of the composers of his day.

[1] A fine soft paper made from mulberry bark. (Trans.).

Emmanuel Chabrier

ALFRED BRUNEAU

I have always much loved and much admired Chabrier, because I have always believed him to be the most living composer of his time.

He was alive, colourful, exuberant, full of powerful enthusiasms and magnificent indignations, from the first moments of his artistic novitiate to the melancholy hour when his creative energies came to an abrupt halt, vanquished by the supreme effort of evoking the characters of *Briseïs*: not in the wake of any sort of decline, but still healthy and strong, cutting off in irreversible and shattering fashion his prodigious gift for living.

Both in his music and his life, this superb gift allowed him to be at once sublime and familiar, tender and cruel: joyous to the point of exaggeration in laughter and fantasy, and good even in the expression of sadness or grief.

Because his spirit was so alive, expansive and unrestrained, I love and admire him now in his work, to which he gave the best of himself, and which will assure him a fame which is long overdue.

In Memoriam

GUSTAVE CHARPENTIER

In a filial way I have always admired Chabrier, and will always admire him. Although born into an epoch when certain musical schools, still far from inactive, affirmed in their works—if not in their words—the supremacy in art of the head over the heart, he made a marvellous protest by creating works which were alive and vigorous, cruel and tender, fearless and joyful. They were like a shaft of sunlight amongst the grey works of his young contemporaries.

It is to the honour of Catulle Mendès that he understood this radiant genius, and guided him towards the theatre, where his original and powerful vision of life could find stimulus and affirmation. Alas, it was too late, for *Briseïs* was left unfinished. Our radiant and good friend has been stricken on the threshold of fame, as though dazzled at having lifted the veil of Eternal Beauty.

Emmanuel Chabrier

ERNEST CHAUSSON

Chabrier possessed in the highest degree that gift which makes great artists, and through which they re-create all manner of things: a strong personality. In his works, as in his life, he was content to be himself, full of verve, infectious gaiety, relaxed goodness and the need to expand.

This originality, which was his genius, was also the cause of the peculiar charm he spread around him. This charm survives only in the memory of those who knew and loved him.

And that is why, while so many other voices are raised in praise of his works, I have simply wanted to remember the many happy hours passed in his company, which none of his friends will forget.

In Memoriam

VINCENT D'INDY

Seldom has Buffon's oft-quoted aphorism been more applicable than to the work of Emmanuel Chabrier.

Chabrier's style is Chabrier himself: his almost heroic good nature, his rich imagery and always unexpected sallies of wit, above all his outbursts of feeling, so basic to his nature, are the elemental cause of the irresistible outpouring of melody which captivates us in his work.

A poet, and even more a musician—a poet of sounds—cannot create except through the heart: in art only feeling gives life.

In that great primitive who was Emmanuel Chabrier, the heart took precedence, as a friend profoundly attached to him can attest: that is why Chabrier was a very great artist.

Emmanuel Chabrier

CHARLES LAMOUREUX

Emmanuel Chabrier, an unforgettable friend, has left in his work the deep imprint of his mind and heart.

His impetuous originality, his superabundant gaiety, his goodness, his tenderness, his enthusiasm, display themselves in dazzling colours on his rich musical palette, and the first act of *Briseïs* gives the measure of what one could expect from this great artist whose independence, faith and integrity never compromised in the face of fashion or convention.

His work will endure.

In Memoriam

ANDRÉ MESSAGER

For his powerful temperament, the captivating frenzy of his inspiration, the novelty of his rhythms and the originality of his ideas Chabrier deserves a foremost place amongst composers of the modern French school. An artist with the noblest aspirations, living always to the height of his ideals, he has written music from the heart to the heart. With joyous and superabundant exuberance, he has as it were created laughter in music, laughter that bubbles up with unexpected rhythms, pleasing and novel harmonies, brilliant sonorities and ever-changing combinations of tone-colour. His thought is a tumultuous torrent which gathers up everything as it passes, pure gold as well as earth and pebbles.

Briseïs is there, though alas unfinished, to show what heights he might have attained had he emerged alive from this terrible struggle with the ideal which silenced and killed him.

May a friend be permitted to lay his tribute of admiration and regret at the foot of this memorial raised to Emmanuel Chabrier by the poet who inspired his two noblest works: *Gwendoline* and *Briseïs*.

Emmanuel Chabrier

FELIX MOTTL

I consider the work of Emmanuel Chabrier to be very significant in the history of music.

The grace of his invention, his intensity of feeling and technical mastery make of him one of those composers who merit the admiration of the entire world of music.

I confidently hope this time of justice will come, and I will then be very proud to have been one of those who helped to make his rare creative gifts appreciated outside his native country.

In Memoriam

Sa jeunesse ne fut qu'un printemps passager
Qui présagea les fruits d'un fécond automne,
Mais avant que le grain fût grappe pour la tonne,
Il vit verdir le cep sans pouvoir vendanger.

Laissons avril sourire et décembre neiger.
La mort inattendue et toujours monotone
Interrompt la chanson que sur sa flûte entonne
L'enfant qui l'anima d'un refrain messager.

Le doux chant isolé qu'emporte un vent farouche
Se disperse, renaît, passe de bouche en bouche,
S'enfle de voix en voix et se reprend en chœur;

Une invisible lèvre au pipeau taciturne
S'unit encore, de l'ombre, au jeu vaste et vainqueur;
Et l'amphore où l'on boit a la forme de l'urne.

Henri de Régnier.

Emmanuel Chabrier

La maigre aux yeux d'ivoire, offensée par Lazare
A l'evocation du Bleu Conquistador,
Voulut, aspic d'acier, sa faucille d'avare
Au col prématuré de ta science d'or.

Depuis, malgré les dures planches où la moire
Avec son sceptre d'or, un soir, t'a reculé,
La faim religieuse de notre mémoire,
Enfant, sourit aux grains de ton magique blé.

Ne te plains pas, ô jeune exemple de splendeur,
Ami qui ne connut le mensonge de vivre
Et dont la gloire est belle de dive couleur.

Plains-nous plutôt, front d'or, d'un or jamais changeant
Plains tes frères pâlis par la chimère à suivre
Et qui s'endormiront avec un front d'argent !

Saint-Pol-Roux.

In Memoriam

Ainsi que priaient les apôtres,
Unis en l'esprit, à genoux,
Nous voici les uns près des autres,
N'es-tu pas au milieu de nous?

Oh ! silence, une voix s'élève
Du fond de l'ombre de nos chants,
Elle s'ouvre en nous comme un rêve,
Comme une flamme dans l'encens.

Elle est semblable à la lumière
Qui trône au blanc faîte des monts,
Où se mêlent à nos prières
Toutes les roses des vallons.

Et nous sommes unis en elle
Dont les ondes et les accords
Enveloppent nos voix mortelles
Dans son immortalité d'or.

Charles Van Lerberghe.

Emmanuel Chabrier

Certes, tu es entré dans la cité des tombes,
Grave et triste comme un vainqueur qui fuit le glaive;
Au bruit lourd de la herse noire qui retombe
Tu as baisé au cou la mort expiatoire;

Et nous restions muets, appuyés sur nos lances,
A regarder la nuit se faire sur nos rêves
Avec aux lèvres le blasphème que l'on lance
Quand la muraille haute est un défi au glaive;

Et maintenant, ami, devant la grande porte
Dont tu franchis le seuil sans détourner la tête,
Nous rêvons le baiser qui panse et réconforte
Et la trêve de Dieu où tu dors, ô poète !

Francis Viélé-Griffin.

Unpublished Letters

UNPUBLISHED LETTERS

As Monsieur Desaymard's selection[1] of Chabrier's letters is unfortunately no longer available, I expect the reader will be glad of the opportunity to meet Chabrier the writer, who is no whit less picturesque than Chabrier the composer.

The unpublished letters collected here are quite remarkable. For the most part they are addressed to his wife or his son Marcel, and give us a picture of an incomparable husband and father.

It is obvious that Chabrier writes for his own pleasure. One letter touches me particularly, the one in which he describes his stay with his friends the Maupas, outside Amboise. Like Chabrier, I am from choice an inhabitant of Touraine, and my house is only a few kilometres away from 'La Guérinière'. I hope that the *Grand Meaulnes*[2] atmosphere in his account entrances the reader as much as it does me.

The letter sent to the Minister of Fine Arts on behalf of Sax is also included, and bears witness to Chabrier's deep generosity and sense of justice.

The letters are not grouped chronologically: they are arranged like pictures in a gallery, without concern for dates.

[1] Joseph Desaymard, *Emmanuel Chabrier d'après ses lettres* (1934).
[2] *Le Grand Meaulnes*, famous novel by Alain Fournier (Trans.).

Emmanuel Chabrier

Friday, 25 July, [18]89
Bayreuth

Yesterday evening, the miraculous *Parsifal*. I'm spending quite unforgettable evenings here.

This evening rest, and tomorrow too: on Sunday there's *Parsifal*, and on Monday, *Tristan*.

This evening, Madame Wagner's flunkey, or rather her confidential servant, came to invite me to supper at Wahnfried. As you see, I'm one of the *élite*: I'll be going with the Van Dycks, of course. I shall meet again the Munich conductor, Levi, whom I find charming, my old friend Mottl, and a whole set of people who can be helpful. I'll let you know how it all goes. Probably they'll sit me down at the piano, but if, as I believe (and as Madame Wagner told the Van Dycks) it's an intimate evening, the *bons camarades* will be missing, and so I won't mind playing: on the contrary. For the rest, I'll describe to you exactly what happens, very faithfully.

This afternoon (and this morning too) I took some interesting notes on *Parsifal*, dictated by Ernest. It's a long job, so we shall do a little every day. I'm afraid I won't be able to get to the end. Never mind, it's all so much achieved.

I don't need to tell you, little maman, how happy I am about this evening's invitation: the Lamoureux will be . . . quite flabbergasted. They're not here yet, but you can imagine how I'll enjoy telling them.

Bayreuth is a real nest of intrigue, so I'm being immensely circumspect. Tomorrow we're all going to Nuremberg, and coming back in the evening.

So till tomorrow: long letter! Your wolf sends you all so much love and more! (I think it's Mottl who got me invited).

Till tomorrow, your wolf,

EMMANUEL.

There are twelve of us at table—12.45 a.m.

Unpublished Letters

29 July, [18]89
Bayreuth—half-past midnight

Performance of the marvellous *Parsifal*. During the first interval, visit the Wagners in their box: introductions and bally-hoo.

I go down: I meet Lamoureux, who asks me where to piss, so I take him to piss. Coming back, the inevitable Chevillards appear, arm-in-arm, very snooty, but it cuts no ice. HERE my standing is as good as theirs.

Half way round, I meet old Le Camus. He arrived for the very beginning, right off the train.

The Chaussons have invited me to supper tomorrow. Van Dyck isn't singing today, it's his deputy: he's rather feeble, so of course Ernest is as pleased as Punch.

In the second interval, I go and look for the photograph taken of me by the theatre itself AS A DISTINGUISHED MAN, and which I'll send off at once to my pet scamp, tomorrow I'll have the one with *Ernest*; I'll send it to you later on.

After the performance, I clambered into the carriage of the Princesse de Scey[1] with the Princesse's mother; I ate enough for four. I've just got back, and I'm dropping with sleep! A toi ma petite femme!

Your EMMANUEL.

[1] Later Princesse Edmond de Polignac.

Emmanuel Chabrier

La Membrolle

My dear Marcel,

Don't worry about your umbrella, I took it by mistake. We were probably both so upset at leaving each other that we lost our heads. All the same I still seem to have mine, and hope (as they say in the country) that the present finds you as well as it leaves me.

My greetings to Monsieur Bidault.[1] Tell him to eat his pears and apples in *tête à tête* with Madame B., there are some young cavaliers there who guzzle quite enough at home: it's no good their cleaning their teeth with choice pippins before their *bachot*.

And now go back to your room, and tomorrow give my best greetings to Malebranche,[2] Descartes and to Papa Saisset, once my indulgent examiner.

Enough of all that.

Your father,
EM.

[1] In charge of the *pension*.
[2] Malebranche (1638-1715), French metaphysician who wrote about the relationship of soul and body (Trans.).

Unpublished Letters

Nice

Mon petit chéri,

We were so sorry to hear that your little bird has died. Mother began to cry, and your poor devil of a father had tears in his eyes too. But it's the same for little birds as for us: if we stuff ourselves like cannon, we explode too. He certainly ate too much, he was too spoilt. We are all at fault if he has rendered up his little soul to God. It would never have happened in the garden; he was always swollen, and didn't have enough air. Bury him in your little garden, and we will find him a little brother.

Soon I will send you another letter.

I am hurrying off to Monte-Carlo.

From your father, who loves you dearly.

              Work hard.

                            EMMANUEL.

Emmanuel Chabrier

La Membrolle
26 June, 1890

Phew! you're hard on your shoes! if you didn't walk on all the flints you find on the road, you wouldn't scratch your shoe-leather; it's first-quality leather, too, the king of leathers and the leather of kings. No sooner do you see a razor-blade on the path, than you have to rush off and scrape your shoe-uppers against it—it's infuriating. You'll have to pay for the next pair; you will have to see the head of R.

Another four francs for your blessed watch, which is only worth three. All right, I'll take it for you; it's the last mending it'll get, I warn you. The little idiot of a watchmaker assured me that you'd have it for the rest of your days if you took care of it; and he was holding it in a filthy paw (his hand, mark you, not his foot); enough said.

Your father will take you out on Sunday. In the morning we'll go and see Nanine, then we'll eat a sandwich somewhere, and finish up the day with the Verdhurts at Suresnes.

I know that Englishwoman you met on top of the tram: she's the Queen of England. She often goes about *incognito* like that: as she comes of a great family, she has very small feet, a fact which has not escaped an observer of your ilk; but it's not only the Queen of England who travels on the top of buses, and please don't talk to people you don't know. Anyway, I recommended you to flop down inside: it's much more distinguished!

Till Sunday, big wolf, work hard, I beg you.

From your father, mother, and little Didi.

Big Didi,
EMMANUEL.

Unpublished Letters

Tuesday, 25 June, [18]89
La Membrolle

Maman,

Everything has arrived, and it's splendid: thank you so much.

For EIGHT DAYS I haven't been able to get anything done, it just doesn't come. I'm in one of my bad moods, so you can imagine how I feel! Yes, I've really been slogging, I haven't written a *note*, I've been hearing one final note, for eight days.

What a profession! And you aren't here! Perhaps something will happen soon.

Tomorrow I'm meeting the Curé of Fondettes who is going to sing me a whole lot of sacred chants I need: maybe that'll be my salvation, I hope so anyway. It's about time. You've no idea how difficult this blessed *Briseïs* is! And it isn't anywhere near finished, I warrant you! I don't want to go mad, so I shall be forced to stop working on such a long and complicated business, then start again. After all, the little that has been done is confoundedly good: there's always that comfort! So I'll work like the devil from the 10th onwards: it's a pact, and I won't budge an inch.

Till tomorrow, maman.
I love you with all my heart.

LE PAPA EMM.

Emmanuel Chabrier

La Membrolle

Maman, I promise you I'm smoking much less, and am perfectly all right. Your wolf is very well-behaved.

Mère Bordier will be waiting: that woman makes my flesh creep. She coughs up the clean linen in instalments; she'll get paid the same way. It seems she lifts the elbow, if that's of any interest to you, and she's not quite all there: but then I suppose it's not that common to be quite all there. And what proves it is that your mother and Nanon, who—in parenthesis—adore each other, have just, in a weather for Emmanuel, that is to say, weather for wolves,[1] set off for that idiotic wood to go gathering nuts; I can't altogether see Nanon nutting: ah well, she'll watch the nutting. And of course they are a very warmly-clad couple of duennas. It may even do them good. They go for turns round the garden, they squabble till ten o'clock; and this morning, with that little air of hers, Nanon said to me: " Goodness, how kind Madame Dejean is to me! I'm never bored for a single minute!"

Your father has shelled out.[2] He has decided to disburse the princely sum of 250 francs, which means he only owes Grandmother 1750 francs. She didn't fail to remind him of it when she acknowledged receipt.

Incidentally he talks about the pain and the operation, which he is still putting off; I understand that and don't hold it against him. If one means to live on good terms with one's bladder it's always as well that the operation to have it cut in four should be the greatest masterpiece of its kind.

Until Saturday, petite maman.

At about four o'clock at the house as usual.

Kiss the little wolves for me.

Your EMM.

[1] A play on the phrase *un froid de loup*, weather for wolves (cf. *freddo cane*, Ital.) (Trans.).
[2] The Dejean couple lived apart.

Unpublished Letters

La Guérinière
1 September, [18]85, 10.45 a.m.

La Petite Maman,

Yesterday at 5.20, Monsieur de Maupas was waiting for me at the station with a brake, and a superb pair of horses. They went like greased lightning, and in an hour we were at La Guérinière.

Trees, trees, and still more trees, as far as the eye can see: and it was already dark, and a sharp nip in the air: no mist except for the hot and vigorous breath of the two horses burning up the road, their ears bolt upright.

Madame de Maupas has grown stout, particularly in the body: she was overjoyed to see me, and very pressing. Then there's the father of Monsieur de Maupas, an old-style officer, deaf, 76 years old, but with a strong constitution. He's tall, with a strong voice, curling moustaches, capable of living to be a hundred. What's more, he's an athlete like his son, and with the back of his hand could send your poor wolf reeling fifteen feet. But he's got a heart of gold, and is as gentle as a lamb. He adores his wife, whom he gazes at a while and who sits in state in a magnificent Louis XIII château, excessively authentic, with turrets, draw-bridges, lakes, outbuildings, offices, farms, 500 hectares of woods. It must be worth a bit.

Just the four of us at dinner, then pipes in the drawing-room, three pipes, two for them and one for me, and no hint of show: and what reception rooms! It is very like the castle the Cornils rented that summer, do you remember? Immense furniture with acre-sized billiard-tables, 15-metre sofas and fifty guest-rooms. Monsieur de Maupas is a great hunter, 40 or 42 years old, tanned by the sun, always inspecting his property, which he administers very carefully, and which gives him a big return: ten to twelve horses, twenty cows, legions of chickens, rabbits, hares, roe-deer and wild boar, because he hunts on horseback, using more than fifty hounds, which bark all over the place. Not an artist, but intelligent, gay and very strong, and last but not least, a charming man.

After dinner, there was music for four hands with the mistress of the house, naturally until ten o'clock: then to bed at 10.30, in an immense bedroom. A superb bed, where I slept soundly until 7.30, when I was woken by a strong cheese soup which I had chosen in preference to the chocolate or *café au lait* they had suggested.

This morning I went to the park with Monsieur de Maupas. There are five trees there, about 600 years old—I can even see them as I write—and they are *marvels*, walnuts with huge trunks, no, CHESTNUTS with enormous trunks in which rabbits burrow, and indeed even foxes: higher up there are other weird hollows which serve as a refuge for entire families of tawny owls, screech owls, etc. In springtime, it seems that these trees provide shelter and concealment for the love-making of every kind of animal, hairy or feathered: what matter if there they embrace, get a good thrashing, and howl or screech with beak or snout? I was rapt in contemplation before these venerable trees, whose roots still have enough strength and sap to give life to small young chestnuts, which grow up under the immense protective wings of their great-great-grandfathers: what power! it's admirable: I guarantee one wouldn't compose affected nonsense in the shadow of such giants. I shall come back and look at them again: it's better than listening to Massenet: these trees make me think of Old Father Bach, who, like them, still nourishes young generations of musicians, and will always nourish them.

The walk is at an end.

Monsieur de Maupas is shaving, and I have seized the opportunity to write to you, little maman, from this room at midday. It's flooded by the midday sun, and I can hear the last buzzings of the last flies who are getting high on a last gulp of sunshine before passing out.

Goodness, but the ceiling is high! I am writing to you under the gaze of a distinguished State Councillor in Louis

XV costume. He has his hand outstretched, as if to say: "A very good idea, my son, to write to your poor wife".

Two people are expected for lunch; a married couple; I'm going to see them and then this evening there's a GRAND BALL six or seven kilometres away, at the house of some *neighbours*.

Here the neighbours are all two or three leagues away, but they meet each other continually. Mme de Maupas promises me 40 young girls between 16 and 20, 30 young women between 20 and 35, then a whole fleet—or shall I say just a flotilla?—of mothers or grandmothers: the orchestra is coming from Blois.

I'll dance the *cotillon* with Mme de Maupas, my evening dress will serve, and I'll christen my new shirt. Tomorrow I'll send you six pages about it. I adore dances, as you know, and I think I am going to enjoy myself.

Yesterday evening, as we came upstairs with our pretty tapers, Mme de Maupas couldn't resist showing me the beautiful pink-and-white dress she is going to wear this evening—all laid out as if it were asleep.

So this evening at 9 o'clock I shall be dressed to the nines.

I am leaving on Sunday. Maupas will take me to Amboise to catch the train. At 8 o'clock I shall be at La Membrolle, but your sister will probably have vanished. She's not the sort of person who would swoon before an ancient chestnut tree. But she's probably got other qualities.

Till tomorrow, little love, they're ringing for lunch. Kiss the little wolves for me, and Nanine.

I love you with all my heart.

Your EMMANUEL.

Emmanuel Chabrier

La Membrolle
20 May, 1892

Thank you for your letter, my little Marcel. Your father is not well; this treatment makes me stupid instead of calming and refreshing me. I need a more stimulating medicine. I'll see when I come to Paris next month.

My head feels so tired...

Work well, my poor darling: spare a thought for your father, who would like to work alongside you all and to have you for long beside him.

If you have a moment on Sunday morning, go to Nanine and say a little prayer to her for your father: she'll take notice, coming from you, whom she loved so much.

Work well, I'll see you soon.

Your father,

EMMANUEL.

On the back of this melancholy letter, one of the last that Chabrier wrote, his wife added this note:

My dear Marcel,

As you will realize from what your father writes, the house isn't very gay at the moment.

Although I had been warned that your father's treatment was bound to be long and weakening before he regained full health, I cannot help tormenting myself, and longing for the expected improvement.

Perhaps next week Doctor G. will change the treatment: it is much to be hoped, because instead of eating like an ogre, your father will end up becoming a matchstick...

Unpublished Letters

To the Minister of Fine Arts

Monsieur le Ministre,

We would like to draw your urgent attention to the deplorable condition of Adolphe Sax, and to ask for your favourable consideration of his case.

Sax had worked in France and for France, his adopted country, for sixty years.

Posterity's verdict on his inventions as a whole can safely be anticipated in describing them as the work of genius.

Sax has transformed the making of wind instruments, and effected unprecedented progress in this branch of musical art.

His is the honour of formulating a law of acoustics which before his time was either unknown or imperfectly understood, and his work as a whole has consisted in strictly applying an exact understanding of this law.

Sax discovered and demonstrated that the characteristic timbre of each instrument is produced not by the nature of the sounding-body, be it brass, wood, or glass, but by the proportions and shape of the column of air enclosed in this same sounding-body.

The numerous types of instrument which bear his name (Saxotrombe, Saxhorn, Saxtuba, Saxophone, etc.) are the practical embodiment of this principle and original idea, so amply demonstrated.

The same principle has led to the production of instruments with separate valves and crooks, an invention admirably conceived and carried out, which ensures the fame of its inventor, which has completely devoured his last resources, and which will in future, once the whole field has been fully mastered, inevitably replace all the old systems.

Due to Sax's inventions, the manufacture of instruments has risen from almost nil to becoming an important and flourishing branch of French industry.

The man who for sixty years has amassed so many inventions, providing a living today for thousands of workers and musicians, has not himself been able to escape the scourge of poverty, that sombre reward of genius, after a lifetime of toil and unprecedented struggle.

At the age of 80, he is forced to ask his friends to provide for his immediate needs.

By drawing your attention, Monsieur le Ministre, to the misfortune of Adolphe Sax, we ask your help in the name of a misfortune as pressing as it is undeserved, and we request you to guarantee him the means of subsistence in his last days.

EMMANUEL CHABRIER.

Numerous composers (D'Indy, Massenet, Saint-Saëns, etc.) jointly signed this letter.

The Art Collector

THE ART-COLLECTOR

By a miraculous stroke of good fortune I possess the sale-catalogue of Chabrier's pictures, with the prices noted in the margin by Madame Chabrier, and think it may be of interest to the reader to have a list of the paintings by Cézanne, Manet, Monet and Sisley, which Chabrier had hanging on his walls.

These masterpieces, which at today's prices would fetch thousands of millions of francs, were bought by Chabrier simply for pleasure, without any thought of speculation.

When he bought the *Bar aux Folies Bergère* and *Le Skating* at the Manet Sale in 1884, it was as much from love of these canvases as in memory of Manet, who died in his arms.

Rarely has any collection represented such a union of sheer love of beauty and devoted friendship.

COLLECTION OF EMMANUEL CHABRIER

HOTEL DROUOT
SALE ROOM NO. 6
Thursday, 26 March, 1896, at 3 o'clock
Auctioneer: M. Paul Chevallier
10 rue Grange Batelière
Art Expert: M. Durand Ruel, 16 rue Laffite

Cat.
No.   Francs 1896

CÉZANNE

2 Les Moissonneurs (The Harvesters)   500
   bought by Chabrier at the Duret Sale on 19th
   March, 1894, six months before his death

MANET

8 Un bar aux Folies-Bergère ... ...   taken out of sale
   (A bar at the Folies-Bergère)   reserve price
   Bought by Chabrier for 5,850 at the   23,000
   Manet Sale on 4th February, 1884

9 Le Skating ... ...   taken out of sale
   Bought by Chabrier for 1,670 at the   reserve price
   Manet Sale on 4th February, 1884   10,000

10 Vase de fleurs (Flower Vase)   1,100
   No. 86 of the Manet Sale

11 Jeune fille dans les fleurs   450
   (Young girl surrounded by flowers)
   No. 63 of the Manet Sale

12 Le lièvre (The Hare)   1,000

The Art-Collector

Cat. No.		Francs 1896
13	Bateaux de pêche (Fishing Boats)	900
14	Au café (At the café) ... ... Sketch No. 58 of the Manet Sale	705

MONET

16	Les bords de la Seine (Banks of the Seine)	2,600
17	Effets de neige (Effects of snow)	1,500
18	La maison de campagne (The Country House) ...	1,100
19	Le parc Monceau	3,050
20	Les bords de la Seine (Banks of the Seine)	3,600
21	La fête nationale, rue du Faubourg-Saint-Denis ... (National festival)	2,200

RENOIR

22	La sortie du Conservatoire ... ... (Leaving the Conservatoire)	1,500
23	Femme nue (Nude)	8,000
24	Femme faisant du crochet ... ... (Woman crocheting)	650

SISLEY

25	Canotiers à Hampton Court ... ... (Rowers at Hampton Court)	980
26	La Seine au point du jour ... ... (The Seine at daybreak)	1,850

PASTELS – WATER-COLOURS AND DRAWINGS

MANET

29	Au théâtre: le Paradis ... ... (At the theatre: Paradise) Drawing	95

MONET

30	Gamins et gamines (Street Urchins) ... ... Pastel	200
31	Coucher de soleil (Sunset) ... ... Pastel	95

Emmanuel Chabrier

Cat. No.   Francs 1896

RENOIR

Cat. No.		Francs 1896
32	*Jeune femme au chapeau de paille* (Young woman with a straw hat) Pastel	410
33	*Le Repos* (Rest) Pastel	1,000
34	*Buste de femme* (Female bust) Pastel	355

ETCHINGS AND LITHOGRAPHS

MANET

36	*Seigneurs espagnols* (Spanish aristocrats) Etching after Velasquez	80
37	*Les courses* (The races) Lithograph	35
38	*Episode de la Commune* Lithograph	45